Clint gave himself four, maybe five seconds before the Moffits returned with guns and opened fire.

Clint did the only thing he could do and that was to shoot out all the lanterns and plunge the room into darkness. Then, he heaved his weight back against the big couch and sent it crashing over backward pinning both him and Mandy against the wall. Guns boomed and Clint felt the couch jerk as it took a hail of bullets. He flattened down beside Mandy on the floor.

They were trapped. No window, no doors to offer a quick escape out into the yard.

"Give up!" Moffit shouted. "It's over!"

The hell it was!

Don't miss any of the lusty, hard-riding action in the Jove Western series, THE GUNSMITH

1. MACKLIN'S WOMEN
2. THE CHINESE GUNMEN
3. THE WOMAN HUNT
4. THE GUNS OF ABILENE
5. THREE GUNS FOR GLORY
6. LEADTOWN
7. THE LONGHORN WAR
8. QUANAH'S REVENGE
9. HEAVYWEIGHT GUN
10. NEW ORLEANS FIRE
11. ONE-HANDED GUN
12. THE CANADIAN PAYROLL
13. DRAW TO AN INSIDE DEATH
14. DEAD MAN'S HAND
15. BANDIT GOLD
16. BUCKSKINS AND SIX-GUNS
17. SILVER WAR
18. HIGH NOON AT LANCASTER
19. BANDIDO BLOOD
20. THE DODGE CITY GANG
21. SASQUATCH HUNT
22. BULLETS AND BALLOTS
23. THE RIVERBOAT GANG
24. KILLER GRIZZLY
25. NORTH OF THE BORDER
26. EAGLE'S GAP
27. CHINATOWN HELL
28. THE PANHANDLE SEARCH
29. WILDCAT ROUNDUP
30. THE PONDEROSA WAR
31. TROUBLE RIDES A FAST HORSE
32. DYNAMITE JUSTICE
33. THE POSSE
34. NIGHT OF THE GILA
35. THE BOUNTY WOMEN
36. BLACK PEARL SALOON
37. GUNDOWN IN PARADISE
38. KING OF THE BORDER
39. THE EL PASO SALT WAR
40. THE TEN PINES KILLER
41. HELL WITH A PISTOL
42. THE WYOMING CATTLE KILL
43. THE GOLDEN HORSEMAN
44. THE SCARLET GUN
45. NAVAHO DEVIL
46. WILD BILL'S GHOST
47. THE MINERS' SHOWDOWN
48. ARCHER'S REVENGE
49. SHOWDOWN IN RATON
50. WHEN LEGENDS MEET
51. DESERT HELL
52. THE DIAMOND GUN
53. DENVER DUO
54. HELL ON WHEELS
55. THE LEGEND MAKER
56. WALKING DEAD MAN
57. CROSSFIRE MOUNTAIN
58. THE DEADLY HEALER
59. THE TRAIL DRIVE WAR
60. GERONIMO'S TRAIL
61. THE COMSTOCK GOLD FRAUD
62. BOOM TOWN KILLER
63. TEXAS TRACKDOWN
64. THE FAST DRAW LEAGUE
65. SHOWDOWN IN RIO MALO
66. OUTLAW TRAIL
67. HOMESTEADER GUNS
68. FIVE CARD DEATH
69. TRAIL DRIVE TO MONTANA

And coming next month:
THE GUNSMITH #70: TRIAL BY FIRE

TRAIL DRIVE TO MONTANA

J. R. ROBERTS

JOVE BOOKS, NEW YORK

THE GUNSMITH #69: TRAIL DRIVE TO MONTANA

A Jove Book/published by arrangement with
the author

PRINTING HISTORY
Jove edition/September 1987

All rights reserved.
Copyright © 1987 by Robert J. Randisi.
This book may not be reproduced in whole or in part,
by mimeograph or any other means, without permission.
For information address: The Berkley Publishing Group,
200 Madison Avenue, New York, New York 10016.

ISBN: 0-515-09176-6

Jove Books are published by The Berkley Publishing Group,
200 Madison Avenue, New York, New York 10016.
The name "JOVE" and the "J" logo
are trademarks belonging to Jove Publications, Inc.

PRINTED IN THE UNITED STATES OF AMERICA

10 9 8 7 6 5 4 3 2 1

TRAIL DRIVE TO MONTANA

ONE

It was the kind of a warm, shiny spring afternoon that made even the hard country east of Del Rio, Texas, look pretty. Clint Adams rode whistling across the miles of sagebrush plains astride his powerful black gelding named Duke. He was headed for old Fort Worth and the excitement of the annual rodeo and gathering of the great cattle herds that would soon be pushed north up the famous cattle trails. Clint had never taken a herd north, and he guessed he never would. He was not a cowboy, and made no pretense of dressing or acting like one. Cowboys had bowed legs and wore brush-scarred chaps. Clint's legs were long and straight. He rode clean-legged. His black Stetson was much too new and clean to be worn by a man who chased the dust of cattle. His hands were strong, but not callused like those of a working man, and his face bore none of the ravages of constant sun, wind, and hard weather. No, Clint did not look at all like a cowboy, but neither did he have the appearance of a gambler, a ladies' dandy, or a successful merchant or rancher. In short, his appearance did not match any of those occupations and the closest thing that a man would guess him to be was a gunfighter.

Years of being a lawman had left an indelible stamp on his appearance: the way his eyes constantly moved from side to side missing nothing, the unconscious way his gun hand stayed near to home, and a never-ending vigilance born of long years when his life was always in danger.

There was one other thing that stood out—Clint's gun. It had an oiled and well-used appearance. The six-gun rested lightly in a holster that was simple, yet designed to unload a weapon fast and with maximum efficiency.

The Gunsmith had given up his badge and turned to what he hoped would be a simpler, more peaceful existence. He actually did earn his bread working as a gunsmith, at least most of the time. Trouble was, trouble seemed to dog his heels, sniffing and snapping until he just naturally had to take a swipe at it. Never a man to initiate a fight, neither was he one to step out of his way to avoid one.

Clint thought it a shame that he had needed to shoot three outlaws in Santa Fe last month and, before that, a gunfighter who had challenged him to a fast draw on the streets of old Tucson. Killing men was a sad, utterly regrettable thing, unless they tried to kill you first. Then it was just necessary.

Up ahead, the Nueces River glistened like a silver thread and Clint knew that beyond it the country would start to lift toward the wild Llano Esctacado where the Comanche had held reign for centuries. Most of the Comanche were dead now, their lands gobbled up by the white ranchers who were making fortunes in the cattle market. The land was changing and so were the times. Railroads were shoving their way westward into Kansas and the cowtowns and trailheads were booming. Down south near Laredo and east over to Kingsville, men with fast horses, wide loops, and hot running irons were building herds as fast as the wild cattle could be shaken from the brush country and shoved north.

Bold men like Richard King, Charles Goodnight, Jesse Chisholm, and a whole bunch more were becoming rich and powerful. Clint sometimes wondered why he himself seemed to lack the incentive it took to do the very same. But while he appreciated money and all the nice things it could buy, the dollar had never been his master.

Neither had the ownership of land or cattle. It was not that he had any quarrel with men who coveted any of those possessions, it was simply not his style. Clint's weaknesses were long-legged, hot-blooded horses and women, though not usually in that order. He also had a definite streak of wanderlust and a need to keep moving along the trail, to see new horizons and new faces. Sometimes, late in the evening as he passed a pretty farm or ranch house, he might look through the window and see a man sitting supper with his wife and his children. At such times, Clint would feel a deep yearning for roots, for a hearth, a home and a family. But the feeling would pass almost as quickly as Duke and he passed and then he would stand up in his stirrups, breathe deeply of the fresh, free country air, and know in his bones that he was not a settling kind of a man.

Lord knows that a lot of women had learned that lesson the hard way. Clint knew that women found him almost as desirable as he found them. That was very fortunate and the only difficulty he ever encountered was when his restless streak began to gnaw at his insides and force him down the trail. Clint had left a lot of women in his time, but he'd always tried to leave them happy and better off than when they'd met.

A shadow, little more than a skimming flicker across the sun, caught his eye and Clint reined in his horse and stood up to stretch in his saddle. He tilted his head back and frowned when he saw the vultures wheeling around and around the hot eye of the sun. They were circling a few miles to the north and Clint's first impulse was to dismiss them as nothing but what they were—scavengers of death, bone pickers of carrion. Ninety-nine times out of a hundred, they would be circling a dead horse or cow, maybe a sheep or a deer. But it was that one time out of the hundred that set a man to thinking he ought to investigate. Just in case. In case the vultures were circling a man, woman, or child, and in case that human being was still alive.

Clint turned his gelding north. A man could not, in all clear conscience, pass on by that one chance in a hundred. More than once during his long and eventful career as a lawman, Clint had saved a dying man because he had sighted the big vultures.

He set Duke into an easy gallop that ate up the sage-covered land. Duke could maintain this pace for a good twenty miles but if Clint really wanted to cover long distances, he had learned from the Plains Indian that the best gait was that of the tireless trot. It was not as easy on the rider, but a well-conditioned horse could hold that gait for a hundred miles without stopping for rest.

An hour later, Clint saw the distant outline of a fallen horse. The sun was plunging toward the horizon and the table-top land was gauzy with an aura of spun gold.

Clint reined in his horse. "No sense riding those last two miles out of our way to see one of your poor relatives, Duke."

Clint knew that the sight and smell of a dead horse was distressing to any horse. And though Duke was not a nervous or high-strung animal, there was no purpose in upsetting him needlessly or wasting time.

The Gunsmith started to turn around but something glinting in the sun caught his eye. So, he thought, this was not just a stray horse or a wild mustang. And what was glinting? A concho on a saddle? A silver fitting on a bridle or perhaps even a rider's belt buckle?

Clint squinted and peered through the haze trying to decide what the shining object might be. "I'll be damned," he said after a moment. "I think it moved!"

A moment later, the Gunsmith was touching spurs and his horse was racing across the last few miles.

As the sun dipped into the hills off to his left, Clint saw the fallen rider. The man was pinned under his dead mount and lay still. Maybe they were both dead. Sometimes, a horse and rider did go down in a prairie dog hole and both died with sudden violence. Or maybe they had drunk poison from the same cursed waterhole. There were dozens of ways a man and his horse could die together, all of them bad.

Clint pulled Duke in and struck the ground moving toward

the still pair. He saw no prairie dog or badger holes, only bullet holes. Two of them in the horse—one through the neck, one through the chest. Big holes, the kind made by a buffalo rifle. The rider was slight, boyish and . . . . Clint stopped dead in his tracks.

"It's a woman," he whisperd to himself as he knelt by her side.

He pushed back her hat held in place with a leather drawstring. She had a knot of auburn hair, and when he lifted her eyelid, he saw that she had green, unglazed eyes. Clint grabbed her wrist and felt for a pulse. Amazingly, it was present, strong but erratic.

The Gunsmith grabbed the woman's saddle by its horn and lifted the weight of the horse just enough to see that the leg was pinned far under the dead animal. He then raced back to Duke, untied his rope, and then knotted its end around his own saddlehorn. He ran the lariat out and tied the loop to the woman's saddlehorn and then he backed Duke until the rope was taut.

At the woman's side once more, he looked toward Duke, grabbed the rope, and thumped it hard. "Back up!" he ordered. "You're no cowhorse but I'm no doctor, either. We got to do the best we can in this situation."

Duke understood. It was not the first time he had performed in such an emergency. Clint had taught the big horse to back on command and it had paid off whenever he had needed to drop down over a steep mountainside and then required a lift back up to the top.

The dead horse was dragged off the unconscious woman and when Clint had her free, he ran back to Duke for his canteen. When he spun around to hurry to the woman, he found himself facing a pale, shaky but very determined young lady with a very big six-gun gripped in her fist.

When she spoke, her voice sounded worse than sand rubbed across a tin roof. "You missed, you ambushing bastard, now it's my turn!"

Clint started to shout that she had made a mistake. That

he was trying to help her. But the sound of her six-gun exploding in the twilight buried his voice and a flashing light of orange gunfire mirrored across the back of his eyes.

Clint felt himself falling and he guessed that sometimes, being a good Samaritan was a fatal habit.

TWO

"Get up," she ordered, still on the ground, still holding the shaking six-gun trained on him. "You aren't dead, just grazed across the scalp is all."

Clint ground his teeth in pain and groaned. He touched his scalp and it was as if a fiery brand was pressing against his temple. It took him some real effort to open his eyes and stare at the young woman. "You stupid fool!" he said in a grating voice. "I came to help. Your horse was shot with a buffalo rifle. Do you see me packing one!"

The young woman pushed herself to her feet and hopped on one leg around Clint and his horse. Satisfied there was no buffalo rifle tied down on the far side of his horse, the woman lowered her gun, but only a fraction. "You aren't the one that ambushed me?"

"Hell, no!"

"Who are you?"

"Clint Adams." He was furious as he yanked his handkerchief out of his back pocket and dabbed at his bloodied head. "Another quarter inch and my brains would be leaking out!"

"Consider yourself a lucky man."

Clint's hand strayed nearer to his own gun but her voice cut at him like a razor. "Freeze, or I swear I'll aim for your heart and I'll likely hit something solid."

Clint froze. Across a distance of twenty feet, they glared at each other like two tomcats about to claim the same alley. She was about twenty, maybe a little older but not much.

Ordinarily, men would have considered her very pretty, but now her face was smeared with dirt, scratched by the brush, and her blouse was half torn away, enough to reveal a well-formed woman. But she wasn't aware of her appearance. Clint could almost feel her eyes probing at him, measuring him suspiciously.

She took a deep breath. "All right, so you aren't the one that shot my horse out from under me. That doesn't mean that they didn't send you over here to finish the job off."

"And why would they do something like that? A good man with a Sharps rifle could blow a beancan-sized hole through you at four hundred yards. Why leave tracks?"

A crease formed between her eyes as the question batted around in her pretty head. "I don't know," she finally admitted. "All I'm sure of is that someone shot my horse out from under me and left me for those vultures up yonder to feast on. I ran out of water early yesterday morning and my throat is about swollen shut. I also got a broken leg that may need to be cut off if the bone is sticking out through the skin. I'm in no mood for talking."

Clint scrubbed his face. He wasn't in such a good mood, either, but he could sympathize with the young woman. No water for thirty-six hours was enough of a reason for anyone to be half crazed with pain. Furthermore, the idea of a woman so young losing her leg to a surgeon's scalpel left him feeling hollow inside.

"Why don't you let me give you a drink and take a look at the leg?" he suggested. "I didn't pull your dead horse off you to watch you die of thirst."

For the first time, the gun moved off his chest and she rested it on her thigh. Her eyes moved to the canteen and lingered. Clint could see the craving for water, see her cracked lips purse and her throat constrict as she swallowed painfully.

"Who are you, really?" she croaked. "A name means nothing."

She was right about that. In this hard country, men

changed names whenever there was the slightest need for anonymity. "First you drink and we see to that leg, then I talk."

"I'm holding the gun."

Clint's head was clear enough that he figured he could draw and wound her before her own battered reflexes responded. But he'd never do that unless he was sure that she intended to kill him outright. And he didn't think she was that kind.

He rolled over and crawled to his knees, then pushed himself erect. He staggered over to his canteen and when he moved toward her he held it to his chest and said with a forced smile, "If you aim for my heart, at least we can be sure you won't waste the water."

She blinked, then shook her head and set the gun down in the dirt. "Yeah," she admitted a little sheepishly, "I guess I am a pretty lousy shot at that. My name is Mandy Roe and I am sorry I shot you, Mr. Adams."

He uncorked the canteen and pushed it at her. "Go easy," he advised, kneeling down and easing her tight fitting Levi's up and over her boot tops. When they caught and would not go over the badly swollen calf of her leg, he pulled out his knife and slit the jeans to the knee, listening to her fevered gulps.

Clint reached up and took the canteen away but she did not protest. In fact, she leaned back on her arms and watched silently as he peeled away the Levi's and studied the damage.

"No bone showing," he said. "But this leg has sure seen better days. Can you wiggle your toes?"

"Sure! I never said my toes were broken!"

"If you can wiggle them without any pain, you might just have bruised the leg."

"It's broken. Look at how purple and swollen it is."

Clint studied the leg carefully, looking to see if he could detect any sign of gangrene. He removed her boot and studied the toes, felt even greater relief to see that they were purple, but not black.

"What are you, a doc or something?"

"No," Clint said. "But I've seen more bullet wounds, pistol whippings, and general mayhem than a lot of doctors will ever see. I can tell that your leg isn't rotting and I still don't think that it's broken. You likely just busted up some of the blood vessels deep inside."

"You mean I'm bleeding inside!"

She looked so appalled he said, "Relax. It'll stop. Probably already has. We need to get you to a doctor, but I think he'll say you are a very fortunate young woman."

"No doctor," she said quickly. "At least not the one in Del Rio."

"All right. Then the next town."

"I'll go with you to Plumas," she decided slowly. "But not until after dark and only under cover."

Clint frowned. "Who wants you dead so badly?"

A small, brittle laugh formed in her throat. "Bart Roe is my father. Does that mean anything to you?"

Clint nodded. "He spent thirty years in a federal prison. Killed a lot of men."

"They all deserved to die. Besides, he was pardoned by the governor of Texas after he'd served his time. It was little enough to do for him."

"How long has he been out?"

"Ten years. A model citizen. My father is a gifted cattle breeder, Mr. Adams. He raises the finest cattle in the world and that is why, at the age of eighty-five, they are all trying to take the last thing he has left—his prized herd."

"I don't understand."

She took a deep breath. "Maybe you don't want to understand. It could be dangerous."

"I don't scare," Clint told her evenly. "And I have a powerful curiosity."

"All right," she decided. "Because I wronged and shot you, I'll tell you the story. But neither me nor my father want or expect any damned help from anyone."

Clint shook his head in amazement. He glanced over at

TRAIL DRIVE TO MONTANA

the dead horse. "Miss Roe," he said, "pride and foolishness are like brandy or whiskey. A little is fine, too much can be your ruination."

"You got a fine way with words, Mr. Adams," she said. "But why don't you stop talking and set me up on that big back gelding of yours and let's get along down the trail. You had any supper?"

"No."

"Neither have I. We'll eat in Plumas. Dr. Thom's wife, Amelia, is a fine cook. You look like you could use some extra food, Mr. Adams."

He scooped her up in his arms. There was nothing wrong with her weight; by the feel of Mandy Roe, Clint judged she was right in the nice places.

"Ouch!" she cried, gripping the saddle horn as he set her down and then climbed up behind the cantle to ride double.

"Sorry."

"It's not your fault," Mandy said, reining Duke toward the north. "But I still think I might have to have this leg chopped off."

Riding behind her, Clint had to smile at that comment. Mandy had courage and spunk, but she wasn't the most optimistic woman he had ever met. He slipped his arm around her waist and she stiffened for a moment and then she relaxed.

"You strike me as a man who takes a lot of easy liberties with a woman, Mr. Adams."

"I just saved your life." He smiled broadly because she could not see his face. "Seems to me, that gives me the right to have a few liberties."

"Humph!"

Clint waited for the rest but nothing came. Her stomach growled loudly and as they rode along with her bad leg stretched out stiff and swollen, he could feel her body sag with weariness.

"How far is this Plumas?"

"About three hours at this pace."

"Duke is strong enough to trot carry us double."

"Uh-uh," she told him. "He might be strong enough, but I'm not up to the pounding."

Clint hooked the back of her heel with his boot and supported her bruised leg. He placed both hands firmly on her shapely hip and then he took the reins in his hand. "Let's give it a try," he said, nudging Duke with his spur.

The gelding responded by moving into the easiest jog a man could ask for. He just shuffled along as smooth as you please and, after a few minutes, Mandy's body relaxed.

"Mr. Adams," she said. "Name your price. I'd be damned interested in buying this animal."

"Not for sale."

Mandy nodded. "I admire you for that. A good horse is a fine thing and one like this comes along only a few times in your lifetime. I left a pretty special mare back there where you found me, Mr. Adams."

"Clint," he corrected. "Holding you close like this, don't you think that means we ought to at least be on a first-name basis?"

"Are you an outlaw or a married man?"

"Neither."

"A rapist or in any way degenerate?"

Clint laughed outright. "That depends on who you might ask," he said with a chuckle. "But I've never taken a woman without her consent—although a few times I've sort of had to talk pretty fast to get them to see it from my point of view."

"I'll bet," Mandy said cryptically. She reached down and disengaged his hands from her hips. "Well, mister, in my case, you'd plain be wasting your breath. I'm grateful for your coming along in time to save me, but if it hadn't have been you, it would have been someone else by tomorrow. So don't get any forward thinking ideas about what I should do to repay you."

Clint felt his anger flash but he held his tongue. Mandy

Roe was every bit as hard inside as she was soft and shapely on the outside.

"Soon as I get you to help," he said stiffly, "I think I'll ride on to San Antonio like I had planned."

"That might be a good idea for your health, Mr. Adams. Come tomorrow, someone is going to pay for killing my horse and trying to leave me for buzzard bait. And I got a few ideas of who it might be and they're going to wish to God they'd never crossed my trail!"

Clint could not help but shake his head. Mandy did not seem like the kind of young woman to boast idly, but if she were of a mind to go hobbling around with a pistol in her hand and a cane in the other searching for her ambusher, she'd not have a chance.

Mandy was tough, a little abrasive, and too quick to jump to the wrong conclusion. But someone had ambushed her and that someone might try to kill her again.

Damn, Clint thought, looks like I might be a little late getting to San Antonio again this year.

THREE

Plumas, Texas, was a thriving cattle town built along the Frio River. Even in the moonlight, Clint could see that the town and surrounding farms and ranches had an air of prosperity and optimism.

Mandy Roe had fallen asleep in his arms and he'd had to slow Duke to a trot so it was late when they arrived at the edge of the ranching community. A dog raced out onto the rutted dirt road they'd been following and barked ferociously.

It startled Mandy awake.

"Luther!" she snapped, "go on home or I'll take a switch to your ornery hide the next time I pass this way!"

The dog, a big hound with baleful eyes, stuck its whiplike tail between its legs and slunk off towards a nearby house.

"I guess you told him," Clint said. "Where is Dr. Thom's residence?"

In answer, Mandy took the reins and guided Duke into a shadowy alley. They rode along the backs of five or six houses before she turned into a corral and barns. Other horses nickered a soft greeting.

"Please help me down easy," Mandy said.

Clint was plenty glad to do that. He'd been in the saddle too many hours and he knew that Duke was worn out and in need of both hay, water, and a little grain.

"You can unsaddle and put him in with the doctor's

carriage horses. There is hay and grain in the barn."

"You sure he won't mind?"

" 'Course not. Dr. Thom and Amelia raised me all the years that my father was in prison. I'm as much their daughter as I am to my own daddy. And if I have any manners or education at all, it's because of these people. When they took me in I was as wild and dirty and scared as a cornered animal. They kept me here for years and then sent me back east to Boston to a private school for young ladies."

Clint finished unsaddling his horse. He turned the animal inside. Immediately, the four carriage horses challenged Duke. There was a squeal, then the hard thump of hoof striking flesh. The four carriage horses retreated in haste and when Clint pitched fresh hay and grain to Duke, the big gelding went at it without being contested.

"Yes, sir," Mandy said, watching, "that is some animal you got. He just takes charge as if he owns the place. Are you like that, Clint?"

"No," he answered truthfully. "I might have been when I was younger. Maybe I ran things with too tight a hand on my first couple of sheriffing jobs. But I learned that most people are like horses, they operate best with a loose rein."

"You got that right," Mandy said agreeably. "I can't stand to be pushed. Why, those school masters in Boston tried to whip me for breaking a few rules. I doubled up my fist and blacked their eyes. They finally gave me some breathing room. I even stuck out Boston for whole year—for the doctor and Amelia's sakes and because they'd paid in full—but after that, I had to leave. I guess there is no hope of ever making a lady out of me."

Clint liked this girl despite her obvious faults. "You're a brave woman," he said. "And you seem to be taking on more than you can possibly handle. I like your spirit, Mandy. If I can, I want to help you and your father."

"Despite the fact that he is said to have disgraced the Texas Rangers?"

TRAIL DRIVE TO MONTANA   17

"Even though it was long before my time, I never believed that," Clint said. "None of the old-timers in the law business who'd come across Bart Roe did either. They all told me your father was not a cold-blooded killer. Most thought he was framed by the governor's henchmen. Someone had to take the blame for killing those Mexicans."

"He was framed. He found all four of them dead when he burst into that outlaw cabin. He didn't execute them. But he was the scapegoat."

"It's done," Clint said. "Long past."

"But not buried," Mandy said. "And then . . ." Tears filled her eyes and she could not go on.

Clint latched the corral gate and stepped up to her. "There's time to talk tomorrow, Mandy. It's late and your leg must be hurting like crazy. Besides, we have to wake these people up and ask them to feed us. Remember?"

She nodded, took an agonizing step forward to collapse against his chest. Then, as he reached to support her, she fainted.

Clint caught her in his arms and picked her up. He strode to the back of the house and hammered on the door. "Dr. Thom," he called out softly. "Dr. Thom! Mandy Roe is hurt!"

The doctor and his wife came down from their upstairs bedroom in a hurry. They peered through the window at Clint and the girl who lay limp in his arms, then they flung the door open.

"My God!" Amelia Thom cried. "Is she dead!"

"No," Clint said, pushing his way inside. "But she has been lying pinned under a thousand pounds of horse for a day and a half. She's in rough shape."

Dr. Thom was tall and thin, his hair was mussed and silver. He wore spectacles and his voice had an air of authority. In contrast, his wife was short and dumpy. Dressed in a loose nightgown and in bare feet, she lacked her husband's composure and grabbed Mandy's head and kissed her cheek.

"I told you we should never have allowed her to go see her father!"

"Mrs. Thom," the doctor said harshly, "go prepare some hot water and food. Coffee, too. Hurry now. I will do what I can for her."

He looked to Clint. "Follow me into my office where I have an examining table. Is her leg broken?"

"I don't think so," Clint answered, following him down the hallway. "I think it's just badly bruised."

Clint placed Mandy down on the table and stood back out of the way. Dr. Thom was a whirlwind of action. He lit a lantern and bent low to the exposed leg. He examined every inch of it and his long, pale fingers moved up and down the stretched, purplish flesh as if they were tickling a keyboard. He examined the foot, the ankle, and when he was finished, he visibly sighed with relief.

"You were correct in your diagnosis, sir. Are there any other injuries that she spoke of? Ribs? Internal pain or bleeding from the ears or mouth?"

"No. She is just weak and hungry."

Dr. Thom nodded. He looked down at Mandy and his fingers absently stroked her cheek. "Did she tell you that she is like our very own daughter?"

"Yes."

"Did she also tell you who might have done this?"

Clint shook his head. "She said she had some ideas and that she would find the ones who did it tomorrow."

The doctor nodded unhappily. He reached down and unbuckled the gun and holster still on her hip. "I'm afraid that our Mandy has too much of her father's blood. She is as wild and unpredictable as a Texas tornado. I guess . . . I guess that is part of why we love her so much."

The doctor handed Mandy's six-gun to Clint. "Take this weapon with you."

"She seems like the kind of woman who will just get another."

TRAIL DRIVE TO MONTANA 19

"I know." The doctor cleaned the scratches on Mandy's face with a solution and a cotton swab. When he was satisfied, he glanced over at Clint and asked, "Who are you?"

Clint told him.

"You probably saved her life," the doctor said. "It's unlikely anyone else would have ridden so far out of their way to investigate. Are you willing to help her again?"

"Yes. But first, I need to know what this is all about. She told me her father has a prized herd of cattle that other men were after. And there was something else that she could not even bring herself to speak about."

Mrs. Thom hurried in. "The water is almost ready and I'm heating up some leftovers from dinner. Sir, I hope you don't mind, but . . ."

The doctor placed his hand gently on her arm. "Amelia. The water won't be necessary after all. There is no need for operating and all the girl needs is rest. Let's let her sleep for the remainder of the night. Tomorrow, you can begin to bathe and feed her back to health."

The woman nodded. She moved a rocking chair next to the examining table and the young woman. It was all she could do to keep from crying when she laid her head down beside Mandy and hugged her tightly.

The doctor led Clint into his study and closed the door. The room was lined with bookshelves and the furniture was old and heavy. The place smelled of good tobacco and there were real Oriental rugs on the polished hardwood floors. He offered the Gunsmith a cigar and a full glass of brandy, both of which Clint was happy to accept, though he would have preferred to eat first.

"I will begin at the beginning. Bart Roe is my brother-in-law. He is Amelia's full brother but they are completely different personalities and temperaments. Bart is full of hell and all those years in prison did little to tame his spirit. Even now, in his eighties, he remains the most cantankerous and disreputable of men. The only settling influences in his life were his son and his wife. He lost his wife while he was in prison and he lost his son only six years ago during an epidemic of cholera."

"I see," Clint said.

The doctor lit his cigar and inhaled deeply. "After Bart was released from prison, he went straight. He came to me and asked me about the study of genetics. He wanted to crossbreed cattle. A truly superior breed of cattle. I was amazed. He had never asked my opinion on anything and, quite frankly, I knew very little about the subject. But I was able to order books and we both became interested in the subject. Bart had some money, I had some money. We bought some European-bred cattle to cross with our best Texas longhorns. In time, we were getting some pretty outstanding calves. Bart began to sell a few for enormous sums of money, relatively speaking. He was very proud of our venture, and soon he was even being asked to speak on crossbreeding at various cattlemen's conventions. He was, quite simply, a man reborn. Cattle money began to flow his way and mine. I was astonished but he was sure that it was no more than our due. No one else had ever studied the scientific matter of genetics and then applied it to cattle. Mice and rats, yes. But not cattle, at least not in Texas. It seemed, for a while, that everything was going our way."

Clint sipped his brandy. He could tell by the way this story was going that something bad was about to happen. "So what went wrong?"

"The cholera took Bart's beloved son. Bart went crazy for almost a year. He gambled and drank everything including his land away. That's when we took Mandy in and tried to get her out of Texas. We were only successful in doing that for one year."

"She told me."

The doctor smiled without humor. "I imagine she said she hated Boston and the school."

"Yes."

"That was Amelia's and my own mistake. But one well intentioned. You see, Mr. Adams, old Bart adored his wife and then his son but he never gave Mandy the time of day. He still doesn't. He wanted another son. Mandy grew up hurt and neglected by her father. Even after Bart was pardoned and released, he hadn't changed at all. He still strongly favored his son."

"Who wants to kill her?" Clint asked pointedly.

"I don't know. Maybe no one. It might have just been a warning to old Bart to sell off the last of our crossbred herd—the best of the herd—and leave Texas."

"But he won't sell."

"No," the doctor said. "I don't care about my half interest in the herd. I figure that Mandy deserves that money and, if Bart doesn't stop drinking and gambling, he'll lose our fine crossbreds anyway."

Clint tossed down his brandy in a gulp. "What if whoever ambushed her yesterday feels the same way? If that's true, they'll want to kill Mandy to get her out of the picture so that Bart has no one left to take care of and support him. The old man would probably just drink himself to death and the cattle would be sold for a song. No heirs, no loss. A smart but unscrupulous rancher could get those cattle almost for nothing."

The doctor reached for the brandy bottle and refilled both of their glasses. When he poured, Clint saw the tremor in his hand. It had not been there a few minutes earlier. That meant that what Clint had just deduced struck fear in the man.

"That," Thom said, "may be a frightening possibility. Sir, I am a healer, not a gunfighter. You look . . . capable. Will you help?"

Clint grinned wolfishly. "You bet I will."

He rose to his feet. "But first, is there anything—anything at all in the kitchen that I might eat? I haven't eaten since early morning and that was just a cold biscuit. Doc, I'm in real danger of starving to death."

Thom showed a broad smile. "My dear wife happens to be the best cook in all of Texas. We have leftover roast, cornbread, chicken, and apple pie."

Clint placed his brandy snifter down. "Then let's go find it," he said eagerly. "With all that and a little coffee, I think we can arrive at some conclusions that might just save Mandy's life."

FOUR

Mandy Roe awoke at daybreak and opened her eyes reaching for her gun. Finding it absent, she sat up quickly and then suddenly realized where she was and what had happened. The recent memories all returned in a flash—how, two days before, the sunrise had lifted from the east as she rode her horse across the prairie in search of a missing stray. And exactly how it had sounded when she had heard the thundering roar of a buffalo rifle. Her horse had dropped like a stone and she had momentarily lost consciousness as her leg was crushed under its thrashing weight.

When Mandy had awakened seconds or minutes later, the horse no longer even quivered in death; the rattling sound in its throat was silent and its blood was already starting to clot. She had raised her head and tried to pull herself out from under the animal but it was hopeless. She had cried out for help, and, once more, the buffalo rifle had roared. Mandy felt the almost instant impact of the huge slug as it punched into the belly of her dead mare. She had sworn helplessly as she fell back to the earth. She managed to drag her pistol out from her holster. But she was not an especially good shot and a six-gun was no match for a big-bored hunting rifle. So she had lain still through the rest of the long, agonizing day expecting whoever had ambushed and shot her horse to work their way around and kill her, too.

Darkness had fallen and her canteen was buried far under the mare's stiff body. She had began to see mirages in the desert, hear the tantalizing sound of a running river. Her leg had gone numb long ago but then had begun to burn and ache. She could not wiggle her toes because of the great weight that bore down on them. Her neck was stiff from trying to look around behind her to see her executioner's approach.

With night had come fresh terrors. She heard animals in the sage, a coyote growled close by, and it was joined by others. An owl swooped across the starry heavens. It dove and its talons squeezed the life from a screeching rabbit. Mandy thought that the ambusher was waiting to creep in close and slit her throat. When she swallowed, it already hurt. She dozed off and awoke in fits and starts. She prayed for dawn and when it came she wept with gratitude. But by the second high noon under her dead horse, Mandy believed she was going to die.

Clint Adams had appeared; she saw his image as if he were coming at her from behind a waterfall. His face was blurred and distorted. She had tried to shout but no sound came, and then she lifted her gun and fired. Only later, did she learn that Clint Adams was not the man who wanted her dead.

But now, as she lay in the Thom household and thought back over the past several weeks, she knew who had shot her horse and left her to die. Art Moffit was an outlaw, a grizzled old cattle rustler and ex-buffalo hunter. His Double Eagle ranch bordered the land that her father had owned until he had gambled and squandered it away on liquor and bad investments. The land and ranch buildings would soon be taken over by an eastern syndicate, but for the next few weeks at least they had allowed old Bart and Mandy to stay. That's why their prized herd was still grazing that land. Art Moffit wanted their small but prized herd of crossbred cattle in the worst possible way. He'd have rustled them except that her father had ear-notched each animal. That and the fact that their roan crossbred cattle were so distinctive in their coloring and appearance that anyone would know they had been stolen if they turned up on another man's ranch without a legal bill of sale.

TRAIL DRIVE TO MONTANA 25

Mandy sat up in her bed and pulled the clean sheet aside. She stared down at her battered leg and when she tried to wiggle her toes, she found she could do so but the effort hurt something awful. Yes, she thought grimly, Art Moffit had shot her horse. Now, he and his shiftless sons were probably getting ready to kill Bart—but not until they'd try and torture or force him into signing over the cattle.

Mandy dropped her bad leg over the side of the bed and winced. She took a deep breath and stood up and hobbled to where her clean, freshly ironed clothes lay neatly folded on a chair. Bless dear Amelia. Mandy dressed as quickly as she could. Because one foot was too swollen to get her boot on, she found a pair of the doctor's slippers and put them on. Then she crept down the hallway to the guncase and removed the doctor's old double-barreled shotgun. There were shells in the mahogany drawer and she smiled when she found her own six-gun and holster. It was still only half light outdoors when she hobbled out the back door and headed for the barn and saddle room where the doctor kept his tack. Mandy knew the secret hiding place where he kept the padlock key. She felt guilty opening the lock but she did so anyway.

Clint Adams's fine black gelding was gone and Mandy wondered if he had left Plumas. She imagined he had. The man had been on his way to San Antonio and this trouble was not his concern. She remembered his strong arms around her waist as he held her in his saddle and she was sorry to think that she had almost killed him by mistake.

Mandy had no difficulty catching and saddling one of the doctor's matched sorrel mares. She had ridden them all a time or two and she chose the strongest one for her long ride out to the Double Eagle. Mandy was in the saddle and riding down the back alley of Plumas within fifteen minutes. What she had to do was simple—she needed to face Art Moffit and kill the man before he had another chance to kill her.

As she headed across the prairie, Mandy thought of all the years she and her brother had lived for the day when her family would be reunited. But then her mother had died. Dr. Thom and Amelia had taken her into their home and her brother, Clinton, had gone to stay with another ranching family. It had not been easy, but Mandy had done all right until Clinton had died of the cholera. After his funeral, her father's heart had turned to stone. Now, the crossbred cattle were all he cared about. All he lived for. And if he lost those cattle, she knew that he would die bitter.

Mandy stopped at a sparkling stream and let her horse drink. She dismounted painfully and drank, too. The water had the effect on her of white wine because she had not eaten in so long she was almost dizzy. Mandy crawled back into the saddle and pushed on. She had forgotten to wear a hat and the sun burned her face. It did not matter. She would probably be killed by one of the two Moffit boys, Maynard or Garvey, both her own age but mean as teased snakes. Maynard had always had a strong hunger for her—maybe, she thought, he still did. If so, that might slow his reactions a moment and give her an extra shot.

Either way, Art was the man she wanted to see dead. She had no legal proof that he had ambushed her, but Mandy did not need proof. Art Moffit was a hunter, a killer, and a cattle rustler now cloaking himself with a mantle of respectability.

Mandy gripped Dr. Thom's old shotgun in her hands. Neither he nor his dear wife would have allowed her to do this, but, then, they were gentle, civilized people. They had tried to civilize her and so had that expensive girls' school in Boston. But they'd all failed completely. Despite the fact that Bart didn't give a damn about her, she was his daughter and his fighting blood filled her veins.

And unlike Maynard or Garvey Moffit, she was not afraid to die young.

FIVE

Clint awoke to a pounding at his hotel-room door. He reached for his gun, and when he had it trained on the door, he slid out of bed and moved to one side of the room before making a sound.

"Who's there!"

"Doc Thom!" came the frantic voice. "Mandy has gone after the Moffits on her own!"

"Jesus," Clint swore as he hurried forward and unlocked the door. The doctor came rushing inside and he looked pale with worry. "Amelia just discovered Mandy was gone less than ten minutes ago. And then I ran out to my stable, and one of my carriage horses plus a saddle and bridle are missing. And there was something else."

Clint was pulling on his pants and boots. Still half asleep, he glanced out the window and saw that the sun was barely up. It could not have been seven o'clock in the morning. "What else is missing?" he asked, reaching for his gunbelt.

"My shotgun and some shells. Mandy also found her own six-gun and holster. I tell you, she's going to get killed if we don't stop her before she gets to the Double Eagle!"

"Why don't you get the sheriff!"

"He was shot to death last month during a bank holdup. We haven't been able to find a replacement. Interested?"

"Hell, no!" Clint growled as he snatched his shirt from the back of a chair. "Get your horse and a gun and meet me at the end of town. We'll ride out in less than ten minutes."

The doctor shook his head. "I don't want bloodshed, Mr. Adams. I don't want any part of it."

Clint turned on the man. He could understand Thom's feelings. The doctor had spent his entire adult life patching up men, and the idea of killing was no doubt thoroughly reprehensible. But, dammit, Mandy's life was on the line.

"You do whatever your conscience allows, Doctor. But you told me that girl was like your own flesh and blood. Well, if what you also told me about the Moffits is true, it seems to me that your choice of sides is clear. And if you can't bring yourself to do what must be done, then leave your damn gun at home and bring your medical bag. You can take care of whatever or whoever is left breathing."

The man flushed with embarrassment. Clint did not give a damn. He and the doctor had talked almost until dawn and there seemed little doubt that Art Moffit was the fella who had shot the horse right out from under Mandy then left her to die slow.

Clint shoved on past the doctor and took the steps down to the hotel lobby three at a time. Mandy would be riding in great pain and unable to push too hard. Maybe there was still a chance of catching up to her if the Moffit place was a considerable distance from town. Clint sure hoped so. The more he learned about irascible old Bart Roe's pretty daughter, the more he sort of figured she had been born into a real poor set of circumstances. Mother dead, father bitter, in poor health and unloving, brother taken away in an epidemic just as he was entering the prime of his young life. Hell, Clint thought, given all that grief, I would be surprised if pretty Mandy gave a good goddamn whether or not she lives or dies.

As Clint hurried down the street to the livery where Duke was being stabled, that thought troubled him a great deal. Mandy was tough, and he admired a woman with grit. No wonder she was sort of negative. Everything she had ever loved or wanted had been denied or taken from her. And now, someone wanted to take her life.

It was three men against one crazy young woman and if

those weren't sorry enough odds, the woman wasn't even good with a gun.

Mandy reached the Double Eagle late in the afternoon. Her leg was throbbing but the pain kept her mind clear and now she knew that she had to do more than just ride into the ranch yard and call old Art out for a showdown. If she were stupid enough to do that, the man or one of his sons would probably blow her right out of the saddle and be done with it.

I have got to sneak in and get the drop on them, she thought. I have to try and do that or I'll have no chance at all.

Mandy remembered the Double Eagle Ranch and how it was laid out. There was only the ranch house in addition to an old dilapidated bunkhouse where the two boys and an Indian wrangler named Charlie One Feather slept. Art, she had been told, was too damned crotchety to live with so he kept the house all to himself.

That was good. Mandy also recalled that there was a spring behind the ranch house and it was choked with willows, alders, and a few big cottonwood trees. She figured she could sneak through the willows, enter the house through a back door or window, and catch Art by himself. Then, she'd probably give the man a chance to admit his guilt. If he did that much, she'd spare his life, take him quietly away to Del Rio, and have him thrown in jail.

I'm not a murderer like he is, she thought. I can't just shoot the man in the back or even in the chest if he is defenseless. Father would do either or both in a second, but Father is used to that sort of thing and I am not.

Mandy nodded her head. She glanced up at the sun and then back at the hills up ahead. Yes, she thought grimly, me and the sun ought to be arriving at those distant hills beside the Double Eagle at just about the same point in time.

SIX

Mandy reached the trees without too much difficulty. It was sunset. The air was warm and she could smell beef cooking inside the ranch house. Her leg was paining her greatly but she ignored it as best she could and settled down to wait a few more minutes until darkness was full upon the land. For the first time, she realized that she was a little afraid of dying.

Off to the east, she could see the sun fire the sky red, pink, and gold. There were crimson-lined clouds in the sky and the earth seemed perfumed with spring flowers that bloomed out on the meadow. It really was, she reminded herself, a beautiful world and she'd miss it terribly. This would likely be her last sunset.

Mandy rechecked the loads in her shotgun. She should have written a note to her father. It might even have meant something to him. But then again, he would probably be drunk and maybe it would not. Mandy sat very still until the sun went down. She saw dark figures leave the ranch house and move toward the bunkhouse. It was time, and she lingered a few precious minutes longer.

What she thought of was her mother and her brother and she wondered, if there was a heaven, would she see them up there? Maybe she'd go to hell for killing Art Moffit but she did not think so. It would be good to see her mother and brother again. Mandy tried to imagine how it might be and then, realizing she was just making the whole thing harder on herself instead of easier, she stood up and hobbled down through the willows toward the ranch house.

The shotgun was gripped tightly in her fist and when she came to the house, she slipped along quietly until she came to a rear window. It was open and some dirty muslin curtains were hanging lifelessly to the sill. Mandy took a deep breath and then she crawled through the window having a hell of a time getting her bad leg over the sill. It was so difficult that she groaned in pain and banged the shotgun loudly against the window frame.

She froze in silence and brought the shotgun around to bear on the open doorway. If Art came, Mandy figured she could not miss. Minutes passed and when she heard nothing, she hauled her bad leg into the room and settled down easily on the ball of her good foot. Mandy could hear her own heart thumping like a rawhide drum. She swallowed dryly, shifted the shotgun from one hand to the other, wiping perspiration from her sweaty palms.

Mandy edged toward the hallway, and when she reached it, she peered in both directions and listened carefully. She heard a man softly snoring. Along the hallway she moved until she came to a big open room with a fireplace and a lot of crudely built furniture. And there, with his boots off and his feet up on the arm of one busted arm of a horsehair couch, lay Art Moffit.

He was a big man, surprisingly powerful despite being in his sixties. She had seen Moffit fight a number of times and he was vicious. Against a stranger, it was said that he pretended to be bent, old, and infirm. Then, he would drive an uppercut into his unwary victim's testicles and finish him off with his boots.

Mandy lifted the shotgun and started forward. She was still fifteen feet from the sleeping figure when the huge dog snarled and leaped for her throat. Mandy swung the shotgun around and saw the animal's open jaws, its long fangs coming for her throat. Mandy had not the slightest doubt that Art had trained this huge animal to kill a stranger. That was a pity. She liked dogs almost as much as horses but there was no time for pity and so she pulled one trigger. Even the tremendous shotgun blast could not completely stop the beast's forward momentum.

The dog hit her and knocked her spinning but Mandy caught the wall and managed to whirl her shotgun back on target before Moffit could react and leap for either a weapon or cover.

"Freeze!" she cried, "or I'll blow you all over the couch!"

Art Moffit froze in a half-sitting position. Instantly awake, he blinked and said, "I liked that dog. You'll pay for this."

"And you'll pay for killing my horse and leaving me to die out on the range," Mandy raged.

Moffit shrugged. "So maybe we're even then."

Mandy was surprised that he admitted his guilt, but, then, such an admission meant nothing between the two of them. "Get up and move over to the front door. Tell yours sons and the Indian to stay away from this house or I'll shoot you dead."

"If you did that," Moffit said tightly, "you'd have nothing standing between them and yourself. You can't kill me without killing yourself."

"I know. I've thought about it and I've made up my mind you are either going to write out a full confession of what you did to me and my horse and then go to Del Rio and put yourself under arrest, or I'll kill you and take my chances with your sons."

Moffit studied her for a long moment. Apparently convinced that she was not bluffing, he walked stiffly to the front door and yelled, "Boys, I've got some female company tonight. Pretty Miss Mandy Roe has come to pay me a visit. You boys had better not interrupt our party! Hear me!"

Mandy heard Maynard begin to argue. He wanted to come

and see her. Moffit grew angry and cursed until Maynard fell silent.

"All right, Mandy," the old hunter said. "It's just us. Now what do you want?"

"I already told you. Get a paper and write a confession."

"I can't write. Never learned. I left school to skin out buffalo when I was ten years old. Never learned to read or write. Can't say as how it ever hurt me—leastways not until maybe right now."

Mandy swore to herself. It might even be true. Dammit, she could not kill Moffit just for being illiterate!

"Get me a paper and something to write with and I'll write your confession. You can sign it."

Moffit shook his head as if in pity of her. "Won't stand up in court, Miss Fancy Pants. Everybody knows I seal my deal with a shake of the hand. All I can do is draw an X. Don't mean a damn thing."

"Maybe it will if you do it in a pool of your own blood."

Moffit blinked. But whatever else he was, he was not a coward and so he stood firm as he said, "You do what you came to do. I'm sixty-three years old and have lived a full life. You sure can't say the same."

Mandy was stumped. She had not counted on this.

Not at all. She could feel hot tears of frustration building up inside her and the shotgun began to tremble in her hands. Perhaps she could make this man call one of his sons inside and then threaten to shoot him? But she knew she could not do that and that Moffit would call her bluff.

"You left me to die," she said. "And if I let you go free, you'll try it again."

"And do it right next time, by Gawd!" he thundered.

"Why don't you let me and my father alone? Let him him have his little herd of roan cattle and take them away. You know we have to be off our old range in just a few weeks."

Moffit relaxed. "I hate your pa's guts, Mandy. And you are more like him than your brother was, who I'd have killed if the sickness hadn't got him first."

"Why?"

"Because Bart Roe killed my brother twenty-five years ago and I swore to break him slow." Moffit grinned hatefully. "Thing of it is, I haven't had to do much of anything except watch that bastard kill himself—first in prison, then in a whiskey bottle. Now, all he has left are those crossbred cattle. Without them he has no reason to live. He'll have nothing."

Mandy felt herself shaking with fury. "If my father killed your brother, then I'll bet it was because he was like you and he deserved to die!"

Art Moffit's face became red with diffused blood. His cheeks blew out and he hissed, "Get out of here!"

"I'll give you to the count of three to come with me and confess your crime. If you don't, I swear by all that's holy, I'll blow your hateful old head off, Mr. Moffit!"

He glanced toward a rifle propped up near the fireplace. Too far. He swung back toward her and licked his lips.

"One. Two. Thr—"

"All right!" he shouted. "You win!"

Mandy felt the air blow out of her lungs. She almost staggered with the sense of her victory. The shotgun suddenly felt as if it weighed a hundred pounds. "Move slowly toward the door," she heard herself whisper.

He smiled. Nodded and said, "Can I put my boots back on first?"

"Yes, but . . ."

She did not finish. Out of the corner of her eye, she saw Charlie One Feather throw a short club. It made a whirring sound as it whirled at her face. Mandy tried to swing the shotgun but she was too late. And as she fell, she heard Art Moffit's galling laughter.

SEVEN

The Gunsmith pulled his horse to a stop and glanced up at the star-studded night. He could see the faint outline of Dr. Thom and hear the heavy breathing of his horse as the animal labored to catch Duke.

Clint sighed deeply. This simply was not going to work. The doctor and his horse were going to be more of a hindrance than a help. I am better off without them to worry about, he thought.

When the doctor finally overtook Clint, he pulled his horse to a staggering halt. "I . . . I'm sorry," he apologized. "I'm afraid me and this horse are too old and out of shape for this sort of thing."

"No apologies are necessary, Doc. Why don't you point out the way and I'll go on ahead." Clint did not need to say that the doctor would be better left behind and out of harm's way.

"All right. You see the notch in those low hills about ten miles up ahead?"

"Yes."

"That's where you'll find the headquarters of the Double Eagle Ranch." He quickly described the layout of the ranch, including the trees in the back and the location of the bunkhouse.

Clint nodded. He looked down at the doctor's heavily lathered horse and said, "Why don't you and that animal just take your time moseying in the rest of the way?"

"I want to be there when the gunfighting is done," the doctor said evenly. "If you're going to put bullets into bodies, I need to try and dig them out."

"Fair enough," the Gunsmith said. "Just remember which side you need to start with first."

"Somehow," the doctor replied in a dry voice, "I don't think I'll be working on you, Mr. Adams. Just get Mandy out of there unhurt."

Clint touched spurs and rode out fast. There was a three-quarters moon and he let Duke extend himself, confident that the fine horse could see any prairie dog holes long before its rider. The night air felt good and Clint's mind drifted on ahead. He went over everything that the doctor had told him about Art Moffit and his two sons. The old man was an expert with a rifle, the sons were good with pistols. Clint figured himself to be a pretty fair hand with both.

He found Mandy's horse tied to a cottonwood behind the house. Clint tied Duke up beside it and moved forward toward the rear of the place, which was lit up like a Christmas tree. He judged it to be nearly midnight but he could hear loud voices inside. There was not much doubt in his mind that Mandy had been captured and he decided that they were debating Mandy's fate.

Clint slipped into the same window that Mandy had entered and moved to the hallway. He peered around a corner and saw everything he needed to see in one swift glance. Mandy was lying on a horsehair couch, her forehead was bleeding and she appeared to be unconscious. Clint had no trouble recognizing Art Moffit and his two sons from the description that the doctor had given him.

"I say we kill her!" one of the sons yelled.

"Goddammit, Garvey, I said no!" the other son yelled. "That ain't necessary a'tall!"

"Shut up, both of you," the older man said. "I got a better idea. We'll use the girl to get Bart to come here and write us a bill of sale for his cattle."

The one named Garvey sneered. "Bart Roe don't give a damn about his girl! Never has. Why, he wouldn't ride here even if we threatened to hang Mandy at sunrise."

"Shit," Moffit snorted. "For once, I'm afraid you are right. We'll have to think of something else."

Clint drew his six-gun and stepped out to face them. He said in the mildest of voices, "Art, I don't think you need to worry about anything but me."

Garvey cursed and drew his gun. Clint swore at the young man's foolishness as he sent a bullet through his right shoulder that spun Garvey halfway around and slammed him against the massive rock fireplace. Garvey screamed in pain and his gun went flying.

"Anyone else want to play stupid?" Clint asked.

Moffit and his son both shook their heads emphatically. The old rancher growled, "Who the hell are you?"

"A friend," Clint said. "Now both of you, stand up and move away from Miss Roe."

They did as they were told. 'Which one of you did this to her?" Clint asked in a soft but decidedly deadly voice as he eased down on the couch beside Mandy and studied the terrible bruise on her forehead.

The two exchanged glances. It was Maynard who spoke first. "He did!" he said, pointing to his fallen brother. "It was Garvey."

"It were not!" the wounded man screeched. "It was . . ."

"Me!" Art Moffit spat. "I pistol-whipped her because she was going to kill me."

"I may take up where she left off," Clint said ominously. "Do you have any medicine in the house?"

"Horse liniment," Maynard offered. "And some bandages for the serious stuff."

Clint nodded to the son. "You go find me a basin of water and some of those bandages. Old man, you tell this boy he had better not find a gun. If he comes in shooting, you'll be the first one to die and your other son will come right after. Do you understand that?"

Moffit nodded. He looked mad enough to eat horseshoes. "Just get the water, bandages, and horse liniment, Maynard. No guns. This ain't the time."

Maynard nodded. He looked plenty worried and Clint figured he could trust him to understand that the stakes were his father and brother's lives.

Maynard disappeared and returned in minutes. "Here's what you asked for."

"Get back over there beside your father."

"What about me?" Garvey screamed. "I'm the one that is bleeding to death."

"Stick your thumb into the bullet hole and be quiet." Clint did not bother to tell Garvey that a doctor was coming.

Garvey cursed long and passionately as Clint washed Mandy's face clean and studied the lump on her forehead. He had seen maybe a hundred pistol-whipped men and, for some reason, this did not look quite right. Then he remembered something else—Art Moffit was an old buffalo hunter and never wore a hand gun.

Clint glanced over at the man. He was not even wearing a gunbelt. "Who really hit her?" he asked.

"I said I did! If you want a goddamn signed confession I can say that I can't write a lick! And if ... if you ..."

Clint heard the slight hesitation in the man's voice, he saw his eyes flick to one side for an instant. It wasn't much of a giveaway, but for an ex-lawman, it was as good as a four-alarm fire bell. Clint twisted just as an Indian with a knife in his fist jumped at his back.

Clint managed to get his gun halfway up but he was too late and even as he fired he knew he had missed. The muzzle blast of his Colt .45 seared the Indian's face and he howled and struck the floor, rolling. Both Art and Maynard dove for the cover of the hallway.

The Gunsmith was furious with himself. The Indian was waiting behind an overturned table with his knife and, to make matters even more desperate, Clint gave himself four, maybe five seconds before the Moffits returned with guns and opened fire.

Clint did the only thing he could do and that was to shoot out all the lanterns and plunge the room into darkness. Then, he heaved his weight back against the big couch and sent it crashing over backward pinning both him and Mandy against the wall. Guns boomed and clint felt the couch jerk as it took a hail of bullets. He flattened down beside Mandy on the floor.

They were trapped. No window, no doors to offer a quick escape out into the yard.

"Give up!" Moffit shouted. "It's over!"

The hell it was! Clint strained to hear and locate the Indian who would be moving toward him for the kill. I sure did make a fine mess of things this time, he decided miserably. Well, Doc, its all up to you now.

EIGHT

Dr. Thomas Thom heard the gunfire and pulled in his weary horse at the outer edge of the ranch yard. He could feel his heart pounding fast but it was not because he was a coward. He had served with honor as a medical officer for the Union during the Civil War and had been decorated many times for risking his own life to save that of a wounded soldier. But he was not a violent or a killing man. So now, he waited until he heard the faint but unmistakable order given by Art Moffit to the Gunsmith to surrender.

The doctor gripped his saddlehorn in worried concentration. Things had gone very wrong inside. I need help, he decided.

Dr. Thom was a very methodical man. His mind worked like a card file but there were very few cards for him to mentally inspect. He basically had two choices—go back to Plumas and try to raise a posse, or go on to the very next ranch and tell Bart Roe that his daughter's life was in grave danger.

Dr. Thom discarded the idea of going back to Plumas because it was too far. It would be midmorning before he could return with help and that would be much too late.

"All right then," he sighed. "You had better help her, Bart, or I'll . . ." The kindly doctor let the thought lie unfinished. He knew that he could not strike, much less even kill his degenerate old brother-in-law. How could you kill a man who had pickled his brains in alcohol and drowned himself in self-pity?

The doctor, the insides of his legs already blistered from this long, agonized ride, turned his weary, stumbling horse toward what used to be Bart Roe's ranch but now belonged to an eastern syndicate. Dr. Thom did not greatly concern himself with whether or not Bart Roe would be at his dilapidated old ranch house. It was all too much to worry about at one time. But if he was home, and he could be gotten sober, then he might just go help his daughter. And if he did . . . God help the Moffits.

Bart Roe, even with poor health, failing eyesight, and bad hearing, was a force to be reckoned with. The man was absolutely unpredictable and utterly without fear. But then, when you had abused your mind and your body for as long and as hard as had Bart Roe, you did not have a hell of a lot to lose.

He found Bart asleep in a cattle feed trough. He might never have seen him if it hadn't been for the man's loud snoring and a half-empty bottle of whiskey that glinted amber in the moonlight. The thing with Bart was, if there was whiskey anywhere on his ranch, he would be near it.

Dr. Thom almost fell out of his saddle and it took him a moment to steady his legs before he walked over to his brother-in-law and stared down at the ruined man. Even outdoors, Bart smelled like a pig and he resembled one, too. His face was long-snouted and horribly scarred, the result of years of drinking and fighting. He was not a big man from the waist down, but he had the shoulders of a bear and the chest of a bull. His arms were still powerful, though they had none of the muscle that was so legendary from his younger, hell-raising days.

Bart was wearing a slouch hat, no shirt, a pair of ancient and unholy pants held up by a pair of rope suspenders. He had a pot belly and was unquestionably the hairiest man the doctor had ever seen. The body hair had turned white years

TRAIL DRIVE TO MONTANA 45

ago so that he looked and usually acted like a pissed-off polar bear.

Dr. Thom considered it a medical marvel tht Bart's body had processed so much whiskey and yet still appeared to function. It seemed all the more amazing how much alcohol Bart could consume because even a beer made the doctor slightly nauseous.

"Bart," he said. "Wake up!"

Bart snorted, grunted, and kept on sleeping.

"Bart!" the doctor said, much louder this time. "You must get sober and help me save Mandy. She's in deep trouble."

Bart kept snoring.

The doctor grew angry. He snatched up the bottle of whiskey and poured it over the man's face. Some of it went up Bart's fist-broke, dish-shaped, snout nose, cutting off his wind. He choked, then his tongue came out of his mouth like that of a lizard and he lapped at the whiskey. The doctor went to the well and got a oaken bucketful of water. He trudged back and hesitated. Bart was known to have a strong aversion to clean water.

It could not be helped. Dr. Thom poured the bucketful of water over the sleeping man's face.

Bart Roe woke up snorting and stomping, his arms waving around as if he were drowning. He piled out of the trough and came up fighting mad.

Dr. Thom leapt back and managed to avoid a roundhouse swing. He yelled, "It's Thomas. I need your help, dammit!"

Dr. Thom was not a cussing man. In fact, he could count on one hand the number of times he had lost control and yelled "dammit." Bart knew this and was so shocked that he spluttered, "Well, my God, Thomas! You really must be upset!"

"Your daughter and a man named Clint Adams are in deep trouble over at the Double Eagle. I think their lives are in serious jeopardy, Bart. I think you are the only one who can save them from being killed."

Bart burped. He reached for the bottle of whiskey and when he found it empty he cursed with the imagination of a poet and the savagery of a pirate. He hitched up his pants and started walking toward the ranch house but stopped. He jumped up and down like a boy throwing a tantrum and then he spun around on one foot and yelled, "That was the last whiskey on the whole damned ranch!"

"There's more on the Double Eagle." The doctor wondered if he had played his hole card too quickly.

Bart stalked back and sat down in the dirt. He pulled on his boots, and when he stood back up, he moved closer to the doctor. Bart was a good three inches shorter but, somehow, he seemed at least that much taller.

"Tell me all about it while I get my horse saddled."

"You mean you'll go and save them?"

"Yeah, unless you're lying about the whiskey, in which case I'll come looking for you, Doc."

"What about Mandy?" The doctor was surprised by his outburst. He lowered his voice. "Why won't you admit she's your daughter and you're doing this for her?"

"She don't need the likes of me to protect her."

"She does tonight."

Bart turned around. In the moonlight, with all that white hair and his fetid breath blowing in and out, he was as fearsome and hideous-looking as a gargoyle. "I been meaning to kill the Moffits before I left anyway. Might as well be tonight. As for Mandy, I want her to live. If they already killed her, you had better ride back to home fast so the screams don't make you sick."

The doctor shivered and nodded. "She and Mr. Adams are trapped in the living room. That's all I know."

"That's enough." Bart disappeared into the barn and returned with his horse. He rode it twenty yards to the house and then dismounted and tromped through the doorway into a garbage dump that Mandy had given up on and moved to the bunkhouse to avoid. When he came out again, he was

TRAIL DRIVE TO MONTANA

wearing a gunbelt, carrying a rifle, and stuffing three sticks of dynamite behind his cartridge belt.

"What are you going to do with those?" the doctor cried.

"Blow the bastards to smithereens, a'course!"

"But . . . but what about Mandy and Mr. Adams! They are all inside the same house!"

"Don't you worry about a thing, I'll tell them to run first."

The doctor swallowed and watched Bart climb onto his horse. The man galloped off into the moonlight. He rode hunched over and the doctor diagnosed him as having hemorhoids and being in great pain. The doctor thought Bart looked exactly like an ape tied in the saddle. In his younger days, Bart actually liked to run on foot. He could run to Plumas and back and sometimes he did just that for the sheer fun of it.

The man was an animal. God help everyone at Double Eagle.

NINE

Mandy awoke and started to sit up, but Clint jerked her back down on the floor as a bullet thudded into the couch. "Stay down," he whispered, "or you'll get your head blown off!"

"What . . ."

"We're trapped behind the couch with no place to go," Clint said quickly. "The doctor is coming but he should have been here a long time ago."

Mandy thought a moment. "Then he must have gone after my father."

"Will he help?"

"I think so."

"You don't sound very sure."

"I'm not," she admitted. "You see, my father is a very contrary man. If he thinks you expect him to do one thing, he is likely to do the exact opposite."

"Well then let's hope that he jumps the right way and gets here before this old couch falls to pieces. I don't know how many more bullets it can take. The horsehair has really been flying."

"If Bart comes, it might not be quite the way you expect."

"I'll use any help I can get at this point," Clint said grimly. "If this wasn't their own ranch house, I'm sure they would have burnt us out by now."

"My father will take care of us."

"How can you be so sure? Moffit is no fool. He'll be

49

expecting anything. Besides, I thought you said your father was in poor health."

"Oh, he is! But that makes him all the more cantankerous and dangerous."

"Well, if all the man does is just to distract Moffit and his boys for a few seconds so that I can get through the door, then we've got a chance."

"If Bart comes," Mandy promised, "you won't have much to do but watch the show."

Clint hid his annoyance. He was getting a little weary of hearing about Bart Roe. As far as he was concerned, the ex-Texas Ranger was just a failing old man who hadn't the good sense or good grace to appreciate his own fine daughter. Sure, losing your wife and then your son was a terrible thing, but it happened all the time on the western frontier and men still went ahead and led productive and decent lives. Tragedy should not break a strong man, it should temper his steel. Clint had also lost a lot of good men and women he had loved. It happened, but the world kept on turning and you went with it doing the best you could.

"Clint?"

"Yeah?"

"How old are you?"

"Older than you, younger than your father. That's as close as you need to know."

"I'm twenty-one. You ever been married?"

"Nope."

"Ever wanted to?"

Clint frowned. "Why all these questions, Mandy?"

She shrugged. It was so dark behind the couch that he could barely see her. And as for seeing any of the Moffits, there was no chance. All he could do was see their gunflashes and . . ."

Clint stiffened. "Look," he whispered. "See that glow of light in the hallway?"

"Yes. What . . ."

Clint lifted his head above the couch and just had an

instant to see the burning firebrand come flying across the room. He heard it go "thunk" in the horsehair couch and then he smelled the rank hair start to burn.

"It's that damned Indian again and he's shooting flaming arrows at us! Put your back to the wall and help me shove the couch out as far as we can. Hurry!"

They both used their legs to shove the burning couch as far from the wall as they could. Bullets were flying and the stench of the burning horsehair and padding was terrible. Mandy began to choke and cough and Clint knew that the Moffits and their one-man Indian war party would be coming in swiftly for the kill.

I've got to stand up and risk taking their bullets in order to stop them, he thought. I just can't lie here and let them close in on both sides.

Clint pressed Mandy down flat. "If I fall, you pick up my gun and get whoever I've missed. Understand?"

She nodded and coughed. "I'm sorry it came down to this, Mr. Adams."

"HEE-YAW-GEE—OOP!" came a long, wailing cry from outside as the sound of galloping hooves thundered into the ranch yard.

"It's my father!" Mandy cried.

Clint heard glass shatter and then he heard a shouted warning. About two seconds later, the explosion blew out the entire end of the ranch house. Timber, rock, and adobe rained down on their heads like hail.

"YEE—YAHHHHH!"

For several minutes, they heard nothing but a roaring sound and then Clint heard gunfire blanket the hallway. It was time to get out before the entire roof collapsed and buried them. Clint grabbed Mandy and threw her over his shoulder. The explosion had set fire to the interior of the house and everything was going up in flames. Clint dodged a section of falling roof and when he finally staggered outside, he saw a crazy, white-haired man on a pinto horse exchanging shots with old Art Moffit. They were screaming curses at each other—both in such a towering rage that neither one of them could possibly hit anything.

But Maynard stumbled out with his wounded brother and when they saw Bart they went for their guns. Clint's eyes were streaming with tears but he emptied his gun at them, placing his shots with deadly accuracy. Both men went down for keeps.

Bart ran out of bullets. He threw down his empty gun and yanked what Clint knew was another stick of dynamite out of his pants. Moffit had an extra six-gun and now he was dragging it out and advancing on his hated enemy, firing with each forward step. Bart, with incredible coolness in the face of Moffit's fire, lit the fuse and held it for at least three seconds before he shouted, "See ya in hell, you old son of a bitch!"

The fuse sparkled as it spun around and around. Out of the corner of Clint's eye, he saw the Indian raise his bow and arrow to kill Bart. Clint's six-gun was empty and he shouted a desperate warning.

The Indian fired. Clint saw the arrow strike Bart and knock him out of the saddle and then the gunsmith felt himself being hurled backward as the dynamite exploded in a huge orange ball of fire.

Minutes passed as Clint tried to sit up and gather his senses. Dimly, he heard Mandy shout and he saw her stagger forward on one leg. She vanished into the dust and smoke toward where she had last seen her father.

Clint sat up and had to concentrate on the simple act of reloading. That accomplished, he crawled to his feet and shook his head to clear his senses. The explosion had damn near killed all of them. With an effort, Clint sleeved his eyes dry and took a couple of deep lungfuls of clean air. He knew that old Moffit and the Indian had been blown into a thousand messy pieces, probably from one end of Double Eagle to the other. He imagined that Bart Roe and his horse had fared little better.

But then suddenly he saw Mandy dragging her father out

of the huge cloud of gray, twisting smoke. The old man was kicking and cursing. His thick, white body hair had been blown away and he was actually smoking but he was very much alive and plenty upset.

Clint shoved his gun back into his holster. He shook his head in amazement. "Well, I'll be goddamned!" he whispered in awe. "That old maverick has more lives than an alley cat!"

With a grateful smile on his face, Clint hurried forward to meet the legendary Bart Roe and put out his fire.

TEN

Bart Roe jumped in a horse watering trough and when he came out, he roared with outrage because his fur was gone and he stood as naked of hair as the day he was born.

"Whiskey!" he shouted, stumbling toward the house and disappearing inside despite the Gunsmith's best attempt to stop him.

"He's the craziest old son of a bitch I ever saw in my life," Clint said to Mandy. "I'd have had to shoot him dead to keep him from going inside there."

Mandy sniffled softly. The flames of the Double Eagle ranch house were licking at the moon and every few seconds another big section of the roof would come crashing down sending sparks and embers shooting out in all directions.

The fire had started at one end of the long, rectangular house, but now it was almost to the other.

"He's gone," Clint said. "I'm . . ."

"Look!" Mandy cried. "Pa is still alive!"

Clint twisted around to see the old man burst out of the last standing section of the ranch house. He was carrying at least four bottles of liquor under one arm and using his other to pour the last contents of another down his gullet.

"YEEE-WHAAHHHH!" he howled in whatever language he used.

"Well, I'll be damned," Clint said with a shake of his head. "I've never seen anyone to match him."

"And you never will." Mandy leaned against Clint and

they went over to the old man who had moved back from the house and now sat cross-legged in the dirt. He was a strange-looking sight, shirtless, hairless, his body singed and wrinkled yet somehow very compact and powerful. He was wearing pants, but they were charred rags and the leather soles of his boots were still smoking.

"Father, we thank you for coming. You saved our lives. This here is Clint Adams. He's a brave man and a good one. He came to help me ethe same as you did. I hope you will speak nice to him."

"Pleased to meet you," Clint said, offering his hand. "I appreciate what you did, though I thought you overplayed it a little."

Bart studiously avoided even looking at Clint's hand. But he said, "What do you mean 'overplayed it'?"

"I just figured the dynamite could about as easily blown me and your daughter to smithereens as that house."

"No one lives forever," Bart replied, upending the bottle and emptying it. He pitched the empty at the fire and then smiled at the flames. "I always hated this family. I should have cleaned out the bunch of them years ago. It felt good tonight. Art Moffit was a scorpion and his sons weren't no better. I did the world a big favor. Only regret is that I didn't have time to find more of their liquor before the roof caved in."

Clint glanced at Mandy. She smiled nervously and said, "Pa, there will be a lot of questions."

"What kind of questions?" He glared up at her. "I don't like people to ask me no questions."

"I know that Pa, but . . ."

"Shut up!"

"Don't talk to your daughter like that, you crotchety old bastard!" Clint snapped. "She's a lady and you had damn well better start treating her like one."

Mandy's hand flew to her mouth in shock and she took a backstep. Bart set his bottle down and started to climb to his feet.

TRAIL DRIVE TO MONTANA 57

"Pa, please, he didn't mean it!"

"Yes, I did," Clint said evenly. "And while I appreciate your help, I think you could just as easily have killed us."

Bart came to his feet and his eyes drew down to slits. He was wearing a gun and he went for it. For a man his age, he was amazingly fast, but before he cleared leather, Clint's six-gun was poking at a spot between his eyes.

"Use it or I'll feed it to you!" Bart hissed.

Clint brought the gun down and reholstered it. "You want to drink yourself to death, that's your business. But I'm sure not going to do you the favor of putting you out of your misery."

Bart leapt at Clint's throat. His powerful hands closed in on the Gunsmith's windpipe and he'd have crushed it in a moment if Clint had not brought his own hands up and broke the hold. Clint pounded with two thundering uppercuts to the heart and Bart staggered back a step. But he gathered himself and charged.

Bart was fast, strong, and experienced. When Clint ducked a punch, he realized too late that it was a feint and Bart's scarred old fist cut a wicked swath in a line right for his throat. Had the punch landed, it would have crushed the Gunsmith's voice box and perhaps even his windpipe, thus ending the fight. But Clint was able to jerk his shoulder up and partially deflect the punch. Bart hit him once more in the side of the head and Clint staggered.

"Come on, you young buck, you!" Bart challenged. "Let's see if you got the heart to match those fast hands."

Clint jumped sideways as Bart charged. He tripped the old devil and then drove a boot into his ribs hard enough to drive the air from his lungs. He had no doubt at all that Bart would have whipped him had they been the same age. Bart was the strongest, meanest man Clint had ever fought. But his strength was no longer superhuman and his reactions were slowed by age and too much whiskey.

Clint let Bart climb halfway up to his feet and then he hammered the man with a sweeping left-fisted uppercut that snapped Bart's head back and sent him rolling.

"Get up and fight," Clint ordered. "I'm not finished with you yet. You're going to treat your daughter with respect or I'm going to beat your muddled old brains out through your ears."

Bart did manage to get up, but he was stunned, and when he tried to grab and bite the Gunsmith, Clint stomped his heel down on the man's toes and then delivered three unanswered punches to the man's already battered old face.

"Stop it!" Mandy cried, grabbing Clint's gun from his holster and cocking it. "If you hit him once more, so help me I'll shoot you!"

Clint froze, then turned to face Mandy. Bart, seizing this unexpected opportunity, unloaded a sweeping roundhouse punch that almost took the Gunsmith's head off and dropped him to the ground. Bart raised his boot to bring it down on Clint but Mandy changed his mind when she put a bullet between his legs and almost gelded him. "Stop this!" she cried. "Both of you!"

Clint thought that was a fine idea. Bart, seeing his daughter cock the hammer and turn the six-gun on his chest, shook his head. "Could you do it, girl?"

Mandy looked down at Clint. "If he tried to hurt you anymore, I'd shoot him dead. But just as sure as I'm standing, Pa, I'll do the same to you."

Bart set his boot down easy and nodded. "I think you have finally been weaned, honey. I think I'll have a drink and make peace with this hombre you've teamed up with."

Clint pushed himself to his feet. He felt as if he had been through a war. He stood face to face with Bart and said, "I don't like and trust you, mister. But I think you are a hell of a man and you have a hell of a fine daughter."

Bart studied him for a moment and then he walked over and uncorked another bottle of whiskey. When he came back to the Gunsmith, he said, "You going to have a drink on that?"

Clint took the bottle roughly from the old man's fist. "You bet I am."

He drank, and the whiskey burned its way down his throat. Art Moffit sure drank rotgut for a man who seemed to have had some money. But the whiskey cut the pain and when he lowered the bottle and handed it back to Bart it was a third gone.

Bart actually smiled. "Honey," he said to his daughter, "I think you might have finally found a man I approve of."

Clint could not help but laugh with Mandy. He guessed he had just received about as high a form of compliment as Bart Roe had ever given any man.

ELEVEN

Bart Roe passed out in the ranch yard and Clint's head was spinning a little when he let Mandy help him search for a comfortable hayloft in the barn. They found a lantern hanging just outside the barn door entrance and when they stepped inside, Clint squinted into the interior and then gazed up.

"No hayloft, Mandy."

She took his arm. "With this leg of mine, I couldn't have climbed a ladder up to it anyway. Besides, there's plenty of loose straw over there."

He followed her pointing finger. He had no idea what time of night it was but he knew that it could not be long before sunrise. It had been one of the longest nights of his life. Clint still could not believe it when he thought about how first Mandy had been captured, then he had allowed that damned Indian to catch him off guard, then how Bart had saved them both and completely destroyed Double Eagle in the process.

Clint rubbed his jaw. Bart sure packed a wallop and so did that whiskey. "This has been one hell of an eventful day," he said. "A few more like it and I'd look as old as your father."

Clint sat down and pulled off his boots. He lay back on the soft, sweet-smelling straw and wriggled his shoulders until he was comfortable. "Blow out the lamp and let's get a couple hours of sleep before daylight."

"We can sleep until afternoon," Mandy said. "My pa, he won't wake up before late tomorrow."

Clint opened one eye when Mandy kept rustling around on the straw. "What are you doing?"

"My leg hurts," she told him as she pulled off her pants.

He sat up and studied it in the lamplight. "It looks considerably better than it did when I first saw it pinned under your horse." Actually, the leg looked pretty good. Almost all of the swelling had gone down, and although the skin was purplish in spots, Mandy had a real nice shape to her legs. A man just had to look at the good one and see that she was all woman.

"Could I ask you to rub it for just a few minutes, Clint? I'm sorry, but it really would help."

He knew he could not refuse such a request or get to sleep himself if he thought the girl was lying awake and in pain. "All right. Where shall I rub?"

"Start with the calf. Gently, though."

"Sure." He took a deep breath and massaged the calf muscle. She leaned back and sighed. He wished she were wearing long-handled underwear instead of a skimpy pair of underpants. "How does that feel?"

"Much better," she said. "Much, much better."

He rubbed some more, and listened to her sigh with pleasure. "Good enough yet? I could sure use some sleep."

"Just a little more, Clint. You haven't done anything nice above my knee yet."

He stared at her nicely formed thigh. "It doesn't look purple or hurt. The weight of the horse shouldn't even have been on it."

"Oh," she said, sitting up and looking at him with a small smile turning up the corners of her lips. "But it did. It really aches, Clint. Right here."

She placed a finger on her thigh, right up close to where her legs formed a V. Clint shrugged and took her thigh in both hands and massaged it vigorously. "How's that?"

"Better. Much better. But just a little higher."

TRAIL DRIVE TO MONTANA 63

His hands stopped. He shook his head to clear it of the effects of the whiskey, and then he reached up and placed one hand right on the soft mound her young womanhood. "Is this what you want?" he asked as he began to rub her around and around.

She moaned and giggled with pleasure. "So you finally figured it out."

Clint smiled. "It has been a long day, Mandy."

"But it's not over." She reached down and slipped off her underpants and said, "My pa always said you work and then you play. I want to play with you, Clint. Don't you want to play with me?"

The Gunsmith looked at what was staring him in the face. His throat went dry and he nodded. A moment later he was yanking off his clothes as fast as she was pulling off her blouse. He was already long and hard and as he stood over her, he admired her greatly. Lying on the straw in the lamplight, a man could not want for a prettier picture than Mandy was offering.

She reached up and grabbed his stiff member and used it like the handle of a shovel to pull him down to her. "What are we waiting for?"

Before he could reply, she took him into her mouth and dug her fingernails into his muscular buttocks. Clint sucked in his breath and closed his eyes. All of his aches and pains vanished as her tongue worked at his stiff rod with an eagerness and passion he would not have expected at this hour of the day.

His hips rocked back and forth as she worked him until he felt a growing fire building like a red hot stove in his loins.

"Mandy," he said softly, "I can't take this anymore."

She pulled back very reluctantly, her tongue laving him greedily. Her eyes were glazed with desire. She licked her lips like a cat that has just lapped up a saucer full of warm milk.

"Do it to me, Clint. Make me feel like your woman!"

She spread her legs and he gladly drove himself into her.

Mandy groaned and her body bucked upward until he was in her all the way.

"Yes!" she cried.

All the weariness in Clint's body vanished and he went after her with a hunger to match her own. Their bodies slammed into each other again and again as if they were fighting, only they were not. Clint pushed himself up on his forearms and his mouth found one of Mandy's large breasts. She grabbed the back of his head and he sucked at her until she gasped with pleasure.

He could hear her labored breathing. Her good leg was locked over his back but her injured one was sticking out of the way so that he did not have to worry about hurting her. Her body's configuration made Clint feel a little off balance, but they were on a bed of straw and it adjusted to their lively exertions. Their bodies grew slick with perspiration and Clint wrapped his hands around the small of her waist and used his rod like a huge stirring spoon to whip her into a frenzy of desire.

"I've never had a man like you before!" she cried. "You're driving me wild!"

A moment later she went wild as she screamed and lost all semblance of bodily control. Clint felt the woman's orgasm rock her from one end to the other like a California earthquake. Once he was sure that she was lost in the throes of ecstasy, he allowed his own control to snap.

His body drove into her with quick, mighty thrusts, deeper and harder until he felt himself unleashing a flood of his hot seed into her throbbing womb. Mandy was crying out, her head was rocking back and forth, and she was making no sense at all but he knew she was saying it was fine, it was wonderful, it was heavenly!

Afterward, she said, "My leg doesn't hurt anymore, and the other part doesn't itch even a little now."

Clint yawned and pulled her close against him on the straw. "If it starts to itch again, wake me and I'll take care of it."

She kissed him happily. "Promise?"

"Yeah," he said. "Now let me get some sleep."

Mandy hugged him tightly and he fell asleep with the smell of her and their union strong in his nostrils.

TWELVE

They sat under the shade of a cottonwood tree and stared at the still-smoldering ashes. Dr. Thom had awakened Clint and Mandy and then hurried outside while they got dressed. Now, he still seemed embarrassed and unable to look either of them in the eye.

It was unfortunate, Clint thought, that the doctor and his good wife were not Mandy's real parents. This man loved her like a father while Bart, now hung-over and snappish as a turtle, was too preoccupied with his whiskey and hell-raising to care much about anything.

"You can't stay in Texas," the doctor said patiently. "Bart, I'm speaking to you as a friend and a member of the family. You came and destroyed this place and four men are dead. The Indian and all the Moffits."

Clint frowned. "I shot the sons in self-defense and the old man and the Indian were dynamited while trying to kill Bart. No court in the land would . . ."

"Excuse me," the doctor interrupted, "Mr. Adams, I know you and Bart acted in self-defense, but what you don't understand is that the Moffits had friends, and those friends would see that you and Bart remained in custody for a long, long while. And quite frankly, I don't think either you deserve or are willing to languish in the Del Rio or Plumas jail for up to a year—if you were allowed to live that long."

Clint blinked. "You think these so-called 'friends' of the Moffits would try to kill us?"

"I know they would. I have seen their bullet-justice. The sheriffs of either Plumas or Del Rio would be powerless to protect you."

Bart hissed. "I never needed protection in my life and I ain't going to no damn jail!"

"Neither am I," Clint said.

"Then you'll have to leave Texas." Dr. Thom looked at Mandy. "Talk some sense into them, please. You know that Amelia and I will miss you deeply, but what I'm saying is the truth. They have to get out of this country fast."

"He's right," Mandy said. "Pa, you listen to Thomas. He has nothing but your best interests in mind."

"Who says?"

"I do!" Mandy cried. "Pa, you be nice for a change."

"Yeah," Clint said. "And unless you want another fight on your hands, you talk nice to your daughter."

Bart jumped to his feet and spat on the palms of his hands before balling them into knotty fists. He looked like hell. Little burnt-orangish-colored curls of hair were stuck all over his body and his eyes were blood-red. "You got lucky last night! I'll whip you this time for sure."

Clint stood up but Mandy threw herself between them and got angry. "Will you both simmer down and listen to the doctor! He's the only one that is talking any sense."

Clint relaxed when Bart sat down cross-legged. "The mystery is that I don't just climb on my horse and ride away to put this whole mess behind me."

Mandy touched his sleeve. "You can if that's what you want. I got no hold on you."

The way she spoke, honestly and simply, cut deep at the Gunsmith. "No," he said slowly. "I want you out of this and safe before I travel on."

The doctor looked at them all. "Uncle Milton left me that ranch up in Montana nearly ten years ago. I never sold it, and Amelia would never leave Texas. I think you should take our herd of crossbreds to Montana, Bart. That is good

TRAIL DRIVE TO MONTANA 69

grazing land and maybe, away from so many people, you'd be happier."

Bart thought on it. "I never even seen Montana. I heard the winters are real pissers."

"You'd tame them," the doctor said, displaying a flattering and clever side that surprised Clint. "You could show them people in Montana how a real cowman operates and what fine animals you have developed. We'd prove once and for all that our breed can flourish on the harshest northern plains as well as down here in the hot southwest of Texas. Once that was done, you would go down in history as the greatest cattle breeder of all time."

"Maybe I would at that," Bart said, obviously pleased and putting serious thought to the idea.

Now the doctor turned to the Gunsmith. "They'd very much need your help, especially getting away from the Moffits' friends. Would you go?"

Clint swallowed. Driving a herd, even a small one, clear to Montana was not his idea of good times. "I'm no cowboy."

Bart sneered. "He don't want no part of it. I can tell he's afraid of the enemies that'll come for our cattle. Well, Mandy and I don't need no sceerdy-cat along. We'll go it ourselves!"

"Now wait a damn minute!" Clint said. "I didn't say I wouldn't go!"

"Might as well have."

Clint took a deep breath. "How long would it take to drive your herd that far?"

"About three months ought to do it even if you have trouble," the doctor said hopefully. "You see, our crossbreds incorporate the outstanding traveling qualities of the Texas longhorn with the . . ."

"Aw, shut up, Tom!" Bart snarled. "This ain't no cattle buyer with a wad of money in his pocket. This is just an out of work gunslinger."

Clint bristled. "I'm not out of work and I'm a gunsmith. In fact, I'm known as the Gunsmith."

Bart squinted. He sat up a little straighter and studied Clint. "You're the Gunsmith?"

"That's right."

Bart nodded. "I should'a knowed after the way you just barely beat my own draw last night. But my eyes are failing. I heard of you plenty. They say you're a good man. One of the best. Maybe that means I won't have to kill you before we reach Montana. Maybe it means you'll earn your keep."

Clint shook his head. "And maybe I'll teach you some proper manners in your old age."

"Not likely."

Clint scowled. He figured if he could keep Bart either very drunk or very sober, they would get along. But it was a far distance to Montana. "This ranch, is it a good one?"

"If you're asking is it worth the effort to reach," the doctor said, "the answer is yes. I have never seen it, but it includes six thousand acres of grassland, a watertight house, barns, and a corral. It's yours, Mandy. I give you full title to use or to sell and return to us some day."

Mandy swallowed. "I'd not want my father to live on my land. It needs to belong to him. Not me."

"No," the doctor said with a surprising streak of stubbornness. "He had his ranch and he lost it. It's your turn."

Bart jumped back to his feet and he would have attacked the doctor if Clint had not blocked his way. "The doctor is your friend and he's right. Mandy deserves this chance for something you can't drink or gamble away. Think about it, man!"

Bart did think and when Clint saw his shoulders sag, he knew the old heller had realized, even through his whiskey-soaked brain, that the doctor was right. Bart looked at his daughter. "If we go, you got to promise me one thing."

"Anything," Mandy said fervently.

"You promise me that you'll never sell that ranch or give

TRAIL DRIVE TO MONTANA 71

it up to a man. Especially a smooth-talking fella like this."

"He don't want the ranch, Pa!"

"That's right," Clint said, trying to curb his anger. "I don't give a damn about a cattle ranch in Montana. All I care about is seeing that Mandy gets a fair start in life. One you . . ."

Mandy put a hand over his mouth. "Please. Don't blame him. And no more fighting. If we are to have any chance of making it to Montana, you and Pa have to work and live together."

Clint nodded because she was entirely right. He had not expected any of this but he was in too deep to quit this girl now. Besides, after last night's love-making, he wanted more of the same. Mandy had inherited her tyrannical old father's wildness but she used it to make love not to fight.

"All right then," Bart said. "I'll ride into town and get some supplies for the trip and then we leave."

"No," Clint said. "We ride over to the herd and leave at once. We can trade or buy any supplies we need on the trail north."

Clint knew damn well that Bart's "supplies" meant more whiskey. "It needs to be that way, Bart."

Bart kicked an empty whiskey bottle so hard it shattered. "Yeah," he said grimly, "I guess it does at that. But I need a shirt, new pants, and a hat to keep my damn head from getting sunburnt. Ain't got no hair nomore."

Clint nodded. "We'll find you a new outfit before we travel a hundred miles. I promise."

Mandy said, "If they fit, I'd give you my clothes, Pa."

Bart looked right at Clint and pinned him with an evil eye. "I expect you to keep your gawddamn clothes on, girl. *All* the time. You understand!"

Clint found himself nodding. Both he and Bart Roe might just have to make a few hard sacrifices.

THIRTEEN

"Well," the doctor said, unable to keep the pride out of his voice, "what do you think of our crossbred herd, Mr. Adams?"

Clint stood up in his stirrups and surveyed the cattle. He was acutely aware that Mandy, Bart, and the doctor were all watching him and expecting some kind of glowing tribute, but quite frankly, the cattle he saw looked to be nothing special. Cows were cows.

The longhorns of Texas were affectionately known as "rainbow cattle" because they came in all colors. About the only thing Clint could see about these big critters that set them apart from longhorns was that they all looked exactly alike. They were red, but did not look like the smallish English Herefords being introduced along the eastern seaboard. Their faces were the same color as their bodies and they were extremely big beasts.

"Well!" Bart said testily. "Ain't you got a single good word to say about the finest breed cattle in the world!"

Clint shifted uneasily. "They're a nice color and they all look the same. How do you tell one from another?"

"Jesus!" Bart whispered in disgust. "I got to take this broke-down gunnie all the way to Montana?"

Clint's anger flared. "Now listen here, you pickle-brained old fool, I told you I was no cowboy and cattle mean nothing to me."

"That had better change!"

Mandy spurred her horse in between them and it was a good thing or else Clint might have knocked the poisonous old goat right out of his saddle. "Please," she begged. "No fighting."

She shook her head at them both. "Clint, you have no apologies to make because of your simple ignorance of cattle. If you knew them, you'd marvel at this herd's exceptional uniformity. You'd also admire how deep they are in the body and how heavily muscled. My father and the doctor bred them that way to result in more meat to the animal. The cows are bigger-uddered and better mothers to their calves. You'll see no 'coat-rack' hipbones sticking out of these steers and the bulls are chosen not only for their conformation, but for their size and color."

"I see," he said, smarting a little because she had said he was ignorant of cattle, which was only mostly true. "But like I said. How do you tell them apart?"

"You start," Bart said acidly, "by looking to see what's between their legs. Next . . ."

"Pa!" Mandy screamed. "That is enough!"

The old man rode off cussing to leave Clint with the doctor and Mandy. Clint was seething and was not sure he could keep from killing old Bart before they reached the Montana.

"Mr. Adams," the doctor said. "I know that this trail drive is going to be difficult for many reasons, not the least of which will be Bart himself. But if you always keep the welfare of this small herd foremost in your mind, then you and Bart will get along. These cattle are extremely valuable. They are the products of the finest breeding program in America. They could revolutionize the cattle industry. There will be cattlemen who see and badly want them."

"Can we sell?"

"Yes," the doctor said. "I am giving Mandy the pedigree papers on each animal and a price at the top which represents

TRAIL DRIVE TO MONTANA 75

its true value. I would hope that you do sell some of the herd so that when you arrive in Montana, you can introduce the best of what remains to their cattle industry. Crossbreeding almost always results in a more vigorous strain of beef, Mr. Adams. It accounts for much of the American drive and energy. You see, this country is the greatest bunch of crossbred people in the world."

"Funny way of looking at us," Clint said.

"Perhaps, but it is true. We are not in-bred like many of the old-line European families, Mr. Adams. We have greater vigor. So does this herd. You will see what I mean on this trail drive."

Clint studied the big, roan animals with no small amount of trepidation. The bulls among them had long, ferocious horns and were powerful-looking animals. Duke was no cowhorse and Clint suspected that a man could get himself in a bad fix if he made a crucial error of judgment.

"Don't worry, Clint," Mandy said, as if she could read his dark thoughts. "We will start off slow until the herd gets broken into the daily routine. And then, we'll set a record up to Montana that will never be equaled again. These cattle are very fast."

Clint pulled off his Stetson, sleeved his brow dry, and nodded without great enthusiasm. These damned roan cattle had just been described as fast, powerful, and vigorous. Funny, he would have much preferred to drive a herd north that was slow, weak, and timid.

They arose an hour before dawn and even old Bart was sober and businesslike as they saddled their horses and rode out to move the herd up the long trail north. They had no chuckwagon, just a couple of old feed sacks full of canned goods that they had gotten from what used to be the Roe ranch house. Now, as they rode across the prairie calling the cattle to their feet, Clint saw Mandy stop and look back at the ranch that should have been hers and her brother's, but which was now owned by a group of strangers from the East.

It had to be difficult, this parting of the ways, this cutting off the ties of your childhood.

Mandy swung her horse far out on the flank and stopped at a small copse of trees set against a hillside. Clint saw the young woman dismount and walk her horse over to two low mounds of dirt. She removed her hat and knelt beside the graves of what were obviously her mother and brother. There, she remained for several minutes bowed in prayer.

Bart paid the graves no mind, he never even seemed to notice that Mandy had stopped for a final farewell. Clint did not understand the old man. He was so goddamn hard inside and yet . . . yet nothing.

Mandy remounted with difficulty, for her leg was still stiff and painful. When she rode past, Clint saw the sunlight catch a pair of twin streaks of tears that ran down both cheeks.

Yeah, Clint thought as he began to push the cattle north, it was hard leaving your loved ones forever behind—and that was the honest truth whether or not they happened to be alive or dead.

FOURTEEN

Clint was bored and depressed as he trailed along behind the roan cattle. For three days from sunup to sundown he had herded cattle. It was without a doubt the most boring work he had ever known. The cattle walked, they ate, shit, and drank water . . . oh yes, and they bawled a lot in the mornings when forced off their bedground, and in the late evenings when they were tired and cranky.

They had reached the Pecos River and were following the old Goodnight and Loving Trail which would carry them up through New Mexico to Fort Sumner and then to Pueblo and Denver, Colorado. From there, they could drive the cattle straight north through Cheyenne, Wyoming. Uncle Milton's ranch was on the Powder River near its confluence with the Yellowstone.

Every time Clint thought about how far they would have to travel, he asked himself again why he was doing this. Certainly Mandy could sell an extra cow and use the money to hire an experienced cowboy. A young fella who was accustomed to long hours in the saddle and short ones in the bedroll.

But just when he started to tell Mandy she ought to hire a cowboy, the girl would say something like, "I don't know how we'd make it without you, Clint. No one else could put up with my pa and I know that, if there is trouble, you will stand beside us come hell or high water. I can't tell you how much you mean to me."

At such times, Clint would just feel downright rotten inside for even considering the idea of leaving Mandy Roe to the ever-present dangers of this long trail drive.

"Let's bed them down for the night," Bart yelled as he pushed his horse into a wide loop around the herd, turning the leader.

Darkness was falling and Clint was more than ready to call it a day of trail driving. He guessed Duke was, too, though the big gelding seemed as fresh as he had the hour of their leaving. The cattle already understood the order and stopped to begin grazing almost at once. All in all, Clint thought that they were exceptionally well-behaved animals.

They found some dried buffalo chips, and that was all the fuel that was available. The grassy plains were as clean as a hen's beak, not a tree or a shrub in sight. Nothing but . . . Indians.

"Indians are coming!" he shouted, knowing that Bart would not be able to see them because of his poor eyesight.

Mandy came galloping over to him and Bart drew his own rifle and seemed to sniff at the air, like an old bird dog that couldn't see but was forced to rely entirely on its sense of smell.

"You had better keep your father in check, Mandy. If he flies off the handle and starts shooting, God only knows what we'll do. I count ten of them and those are rifles, not bows and arrows they are carrying."

Mandy nodded. They both rode over to Bart and the girl said, "I want you to control your temper, Pa. This is their land we are crossing. We can afford to pay something."

"The hell I will!"

Clint took a deep breath. "I'm going to tell you this just once, Bart. Our lives are worth more than a beef or two that they might want in return for safe passage. I'm not going to let you endanger us needlessly to save a goddamn cow."

"They are mine to give and to keep! You try to give one away and I'll put a bullet through you, and then the first

TRAIL DRIVE TO MONTANA 79

Indian who steps out of line!"

Clint looked away. This old man obviously did not care about anyone else's life. "Just let me do the talking," he said, "and try to keep your trap shut."

Bart's mouth crimped down at the corners and he glared at Clint but said nothing as the Gunsmith rode out to greet the Comanche warriors. He could see that they were very thin, though their horses were slick and fat from the good spring grass.

The Gunsmith stopped about twenty feet from the Indians, who studied him with cold, unforgiving eyes. The chief, a tall, broad-shouldered Indian wearing a cavalryman's blue tunic and gold buttons and soft leather pants, rode forward a few more paces. He raised the flat of his hand in the traditional gesture of peace. That was good, but his braves looked hungry and mean.

The chief had obviously dealt with many Texas cattle herds and had learned a few halting but effective Enlish sentences. "You come Indian land. Sky, grass belong to Comanche."

"Yes," Clint said, grinning broadly. "Thank you."

"Comanche no want thanks. Comanche want beeves."

"One beef," Clint said with a frozen smile.

"Ten beef," the Comanche leader growled. "Or we scalp."

Clint felt his hair stand up on end. He had expected some friendly or even not so friendly dickering but not an ultimatum like this. He tried to glower at the man but his fiercest look seemed to have no effect at all. "Two beef," he said in a voice that sounded tough.

"No goddamn beef!" Bart suddenly shouted. "I told you that. Tell these heathens to get the hell outa here!"

Even as Clint watched, he saw the Comanche stiffen as they perceived the insult without needing to understand Bart's hot words. "Whoa up!" he shouted. "Peace, my Indian brothers!"

But the Comanche had turned their attention to Bart, and

Clint knew that the old man was about to start a war that could not be won. So the Gunsmith did the only thing he could do and that was to rein Duke around and drive in his spurs. The big gelding leapt forward and Clint drew his gun and, as he swept past Bart, he brought his Colt .45 sweeping downward in a tight arc that terminated against Bart's bald pate.

The man dropped from his horse like a sack of stones and hit the ground unmoving. "Clint!" Mandy cried, racing to her father. "You didn't need to do that."

"The hell I didn't," Clint said, turning Duke around and holding up three fingers to the startled but still impassive Comanche. "Three beeves."

The Comanche leader held up seven fingers. After a few minutes of finger games, he and Clint finally settled at five. Clint let the braves take whichever cattle they wanted and drove them off into the rolling, grassy hills. He rode out to the edge of the herd and listened to the seven Indian beeves bawling for their herd mates. It made Clint kind of sad to think that at least of couple of them would end up on the end of a sharp stick over a hot fire before midnight.

"He's still out cold," Mandy said angrily. "You hit him so hard he might never wake up. And if he does, it will be without his senses."

"He'll wake up," Clint said, "and he'll have no more brain damage than he has already inflicted upon himself with the whiskey. I've been forced to pistol-whip a lot of men in my time, and not one of them has ever gone to boot hill or the lunatic bin."

She seemed slightly mollified. "I still wish you hadn't hit him."

"He was dead set on getting us murdered and scalped. I could almost see those Comanche thinking about how nice it would be to have all one hundred of your cattle. I did what I had to do and there is still one thing left."

"What . . . what are you doing to him!"

"Hog-tying him for the night. I'm not about to lose sleep

worrying whether or not he comes after me in dark."

"But . . ."

"Mandy," Clint said, taking her hand and leading her out onto the prairie. "Why don't we sit down and enjoy the sunset together and then enjoy each other tonight."

"But the cattle. We have to ride night watch!"

Clint drew her into his arms. "Listen to the herd bawling and carrying on. Those cattle understand that seven of their number were being taken for slaughter. I sense that much even though I don't know a thing about cows. With Comanche in the neighborhood, you couldn't stampede the rest of them with a cannon."

"Are you sure?"

He kissed her and she responded, but still tentatively. "Yes," he said, "I am very sure."

Mandy apparently decided he was right, for she sat down on the grass and then stretched out and lifted her arms for the Gunsmith. "I guess we ought to take advantage of the opportunity while we can."

Clint smiled and settled down beside her to watch the last of the day fade. At least for the remainder of the night, things were going to be just fine.

It was tomorrow morning when he had to untie Bart that Clint was worried about. That, and the day to come. Maybe it was just his imagination, but he thought he had detected the glint of metal far back on their trail. That could very well mean that they were being followed.

The only ones that Clint could think of that would follow them would be friends of the Moffits and Double Eagle. Men coming bent on revenge and stealing this prized herd of crossbred cattle. Clint figured that he had sort of grown fond of these roan critters. It had bothered him to give seven of them to the Comanche, though he knew he had been given little choice.

They watched the sun set fully, and when it had melted into the western horizon like a dollop of butter on an iron griddle, Clint took Mandy into his arms. He unbuttoned her blouse as she rubbed up against him with rising anticipation.

Clint forced out the worrisome thoughts of tomorrow and decided there was no sense at all in telling Mandy about what might await at daybreak.

No sense at all, he thought as he crushed her soft, eager body to his own.

FIFTEEN

Clint awoke in the night feeling that something was wrong. His inner alarm had rarely misguided him over his long and illustrious lawman's career and he had never ignored it.

He moved very slowly just in case someone was close enough to see his shadowy form in the moonlight. His hand brought his gun up and he rolled over onto his belly. Beside him, Mandy slept heavily, her body spent by their long and ardent session of love-making.

The Gunsmith looked to see Duke standing about twenty feet away, and the big gelding's ears were turned straight forward. The horse's sense of smell, sight, and hearing were all far superior to his own and Clint allowed the animal to guide the direction of his own attention.

He could see nothing but that was not surprising because this prairie was rolling grassland. There were dozens of low hills behind which an entire war party of Indians could hide—or a group of men committed to murder and the theft of the crossbred herd.

Clint listened hard for the nicker of another horse, the metallic click of a shod hoof striking rock, the creak of dry saddle leather. He heard nothing. Yet, the alarm he felt was growing stronger and Duke was definitely interested in something out there.

The Gunsmith sat up. He slipped on his pants but decided

not to pull on his boots. He reached for his shirt, then buckled on his gunbelt and leaned close to the woman sleeping beside him.

"Mandy," he whispered, "wake up!"

She came awake instantly and sleepily reached for him thinking he wanted her again. Clint smiled. "Mandy, I think we have trouble close by. We need to be ready."

She blinked and followed his glance toward the southeast where Duke was looking so intently. "The Comanche again?" she asked, pulling on her own clothes.

"I don't think so."

"Then . . ."

"I don't know. It could be friends of the Moffits or a band of Comancheros. It could even be some wild horses or a passing cowboy on his way back to Texas. I just don't know. But it makes sense to find out. I think you ought to go untie your father and tell him we have some company."

Mandy nodded. "Where are you going?"

Clint slipped his Winchester out of his saddle scabbard. "I want to walk up to that hill yonder and take a little peek. I'll be back soon."

"Be careful."

The Gunsmith nodded. "Honey, between the rifle and my six-gun, I have enough ammunition to take on a crowd out there if it's necessary."

"Why don't you let me come with you? I'll untie my pa and then . . ."

"No," he said quickly. "I think I'd feel better doing this alone. Just make him understand what could be happening before he comes completely awake and starts bellowing or cussing out loud. If we have visitors, we don't want them to know we're expecting company."

Mandy nodded. "Maybe I should gag him first."

"I didn't want to suggest that but it might be best."

"Then I'll do it," she decided out loud. "For all of us."

Clint left her to awaken her father. Bart was going to be

a handful and Clint did not envy her task even a little bit.

The Gunsmith moved at a running crouch with his bare head down. He kept to the low parts of the ground and when he reached the hill he wanted, he slowed and progressed very carefully. When he neared its summit, he dropped down to his hands and knees and crawled until he could see the moonlit vista that stretched out before him.

They were lying in wait, at least ten men and their horses. They had no reason to worry about being seen, for they had found a small stream in the middle of a large depression of ground. Had it not been for the fact that there was a full moon and Clint could count the number of cigarette butts that glowed, he would never have noticed any of them. But now, they were so close he could hear their low but indistinguishable conversation.

Clint's first reaction was to circle around behind and try to get the drop on them. But the more he considered how little cover there was in that huge dish of earth where they were camped, the more he knew that it would be almost impossible to sneak up on them. Besides, the chances were slim to nothing that he could convince ten men to surrender peaceably. The Gunsmith flattened to the ground and tried to conjure up a better idea.

He studied the moon and the stars and reckoned that daybreak was less than two hours away. He had few doubts that these men planned to attack at first light.

Clint eased off the hilltop and went striding back to the herd and his camp. He stepped on a couple of sharp rocks that damned near lamed him, and vowed that he would put his boots on the moment he reached them.

"That's far enough, you conniving skunk!" Bart hissed, with his gun trained on Clint's heart. "Just raise your hands and I'll take your guns."

"Listen, dammit!" Clint said through clenched teeth. "There are ten outlaws just one hill over and they mean to steal the herd and probably shoot us at the same time."

"Pa, you need to listen to him!" Mandy pleaded. "Clint, I'm sorry. He promised he'd behave and then when I untied him, he . . ."

"Never mind," Clint said. His hand was at his side. "Mister, I am dead tired of fooling around with you. We have a herd to get to Montana and we can't do it pulling in two directions. So if you have a mind to squeeze that trigger, then you better make your first bullet strike me dead center because I'll drill you through the heart so fast you won't know what hit you."

Bart's hand shook. He squinted myopically and stretched the gun out toward Clint. But he could not quite pull the trigger. Clint saw indecision in the man's ruined face.

Bart's eyes narrowed into slits and he lowered his gun. "All right," he said. "Who are they?"

"I don't know. But they want the herd and they mean to attack at dawn."

"Let's go kill 'em right now, then!"

"No," Clint said. "The odds are still out of balance and I have a better idea. Let's stampede the cattle over the top of them. They're down in a bowl and their horses are unsaddled and hobbled to graze. They won't have time to get out if we do it right."

Bart liked that idea right off the bat. Clint could tell he did because he holstered his six-gun and grinned. "Let's do 'er, then!"

"First, we shake hands and agree that, from here to Montana, we work together."

"You shouldn't have pistol-whipped me," Bart snarled.

"You gave me no choice. The Comanche would have taken the entire herd in another five minutes, and maybe our scalps with it."

"How many did you give them?"

"Five."

Bart actually winced as if in severe pain. "Good God, man! You should have gotten them down to no more than three!"

"Sorry," Clint said tightly. "But why don't we concentrate on sending the remaining ninety-three or so right down our neighbor's throats."

Mandy was already starting to saddle her horse and Clint went to do the same. In less than five minutes, they were all on horseback and riding toward the crossbred cattle.

Clint pulled off his Stetson and hissed, "Yahhh, cows! Get up!"

Mandy and Bart were doing the same and the roan beasts clambered to their feet with sullen reluctance. They did not understand why they were being awakened so early. Even so, they moved out in the right direction and when Clint and the others started popping them with the ends of their lariats, the cattle broke into a run. Their hooves bit deep into the rich grass and they moved almost soundlessly toward the cowboys who waited in the darkness just beyond. By the time the crossbreds hit the crest of the last hill, they were feeling very much abused and very angry.

Clint almost laughed aloud. He sure would not want to be one of the ten who waited. They were in for one hell of a rude surprise.

SIXTEEN

Clint swung Duke away from the herd and the big gelding shot around the hill. What Clint wanted to do was to make sure none of the riders escaped. If that meant he would have to kill them to prevent that from happening, then he would do so without hesitation. The ten unsuspecting men just beyond the hill were killers and cattle rustlers and, when bullets started to singing, no quarter would be asked or given.

Because Duke had a longer distance to cover, Clint let the animal run flat out, and by the time he rounded the hill and headed toward the rustler's camp, he could already hear the first blasts of gunfire to split the night.

The camp was only two hundred yards ahead and as he raced toward it, he could see the complete panic the onrushing herd had already created. Cowboys were shouting wildly at each other. Some men were attempting to pull the hobbles off their horses and saddle their plunging animals while others were taking a stand and beginning to return fire. A few lost their nerve completely and were engaged in a headlong foot-race across the bowl of earth in a desperate attempt to get out of the way of the stampede.

Clint concentrated on the men who were trying to escape on horseback. He fired at one and the man grabbed his arm with a yelp and took off running on foot. Another forgot his horse and opened fire with his handgun. Clint snapped off two bullets and the man went down before the onrushing herd.

The cattle struck the camp and everything went flying. Men, hobbled horses, everything! One moment there was only a murky picture of chaos, the next moment even that was obliterated in a sea of plunging hide and horn.

"YEE—YAHHHHHH!" Bart howled, head thrown back toward the moon as he fired his gun at the stars.

Someone blew his hat off and Bart stopped his lusty yell long enough to turn a few dozen head of cattle at him. The outlaw screamed as he vanished under the plunging beasts. There were a few more shots and then the herd was sweeping out of the bowl racing north with Mandy and Bart in full pursuit.

Clint went to round up the ones that had tried to escape on foot.

It was easy. There were only three of them and they were soon overtaken without a fight. "Pitch your guns out on the prairie and grab a dying star," Clint ordered.

The trio of exhausted foot-racers were in no shape to argue. "Who are you?" Clint demanded.

They did not reply. Had he been alone, the Gunsmith might have shot the big toe off one of them and they'd all have babbled like crazy, but he decided that the questioning could wait for Bart and Mandy's presence.

"All right," he said, "let's see how fast you can run back to the camp."

When they again refused, Clint set a couple of bullets at their heels and, considering they were already badly winded, the three would-be cattle rustlers showed an amazing ability to sprint.

Mandy, Bart, and the herd returned just after sunrise. They appeared tired but well pleased with the course of recent events—and Clint figured they had a right to be.

"I say we hang them," Bart declared, the barrel of his six-gun moving from one to another as the three men squirmed nervously.

"Maybe we should find out who they are first," Clint said.

"We know that." Mandy took a deep breath. "They are all cousins of the Moffits."

"That's why we should hang them," Bart said.

"You let us go free, we'll never cause you no more trouble! I swear we won't, Mr. Roe. I swear it to God!"

"Don't swear at him, Son. You'll be a-meetin' the Almighty before noon."

The man dropped to his knees in supplication. "Oh, please don't hang us."

"Back on your feet," Clint said, his stomach turning to see any man reduced to shamelessly begging for his life. "You'll not hang."

"The hell you say!" Bart raged.

Clint stiffened. "They ran rather than tried to fight. They were out of it all the way."

"Not the one that you winged in the arm!"

Clint looked at the man. He was going to be all right. It was just a flesh wound. "You boys showed how fast you can run, now you're going to find out how far you can walk."

Bart's mouth crimped but he said nothing. "The damned Comanche will find and kill them."

"Probably," Clint said. "Unless they hide in the day and travel mostly at night."

"Hide in the day!" one of them screamed. "Where? There ain't no place to hide out here!"

"Dig a hole like any other varmints would!" Bart crowed happily. He was suddenly enjoying himself.

"But . . ."

Mandy cut him off. "You had best run out of here before we change our minds. You intended to kill us at first light. I have little use for any of you and think that we are being mighty generous by at least giving you a chance you wouldn't have given to us."

Clint nodded. "Well put, Mandy. Gents, with luck and pluck, you can be back in Texas in just a few days and in Del Rio in a couple of weeks."

"At least give us our guns!"

Clint, Mandy, and Bart laughed outright as they wheeled their horses around and gathered the cattle and as many of the outlaws' horses as could be found fit to travel. Extra horses could be a blessing. Maybe next time they came across Indians, they could trade passage for horses instead of the prized cattle.

"I'm glad we let them live," Mandy said, turning in her saddle at the lip of the depression and staring down at the forlorn-looking men. "This way, however it works out is up to them and God, not us."

"That's right," Clint said. "And I can hear them shouting his name."

Mandy chuckled, "In vain," she said. "But even so, I still sort of hope they make it back to Texas alive."

"You've got too soft a heart," Clint told her, first making sure that old Bart was not in hearing range, "but it goes with the rest of you and I like that fine."

"I can tell," she replied with a wink and a toss of her pretty hair. "So let's figure out how we can get together again tonight without Pa catching and skinning the both of us alive."

Clint nodded. It was still not eight o'clock in the morning and a long, hard ride stood between them and the next sundown. Finding a way to love up Mandy tonight would give him something pleasant and challenging to think about.

SEVENTEEN

That night Bart was feeling his age and he went to sleep right after sundown. Clint grinned wolfishly at Mandy and she smiled back in a way that left little doubt that their minds were moving in exactly the same direction.

They waited nearly an hour before the embers of their little campfire died down and Bart's snoring was deep and even. Then, Clint picked up his bedroll and took Mandy's arm. They sauntered out near the herd and settled down to enjoy each other.

"Clint?" she asked, as he pulled her close and nibbled at her ear.

"Yeah?"

"Do you respect me?"

Clint stiffened and then he groaned. That was the kind of question that usually preceded an entire night of constant reassurances that rarely were convincing. But he did respect Mandy and he had to answer.

"Sure I do, honey. The first time I saw you, pinned under your horse, it almost broke my heart to see such a beautiful girl hurt like that."

"What has being pretty or not have to do with respect?"

"I respect beauty."

"Hmmm." She had to think on that for a minute. "Okay," she said, pushing his hand gently away as he tried to slip it into her blouse. "But . . . but there's more to me than just . . . you know. Don't you?" She was almost pleading.

It was getting serious and the desperation in her voice told the Gunsmith that there was no easy way to dodge this sudden attack of conscience or lack of respectability that Mandy must be feeling.

"Of course there is!" Clint pulled back and looked at her in the moonlight. "I respect the way you love that miserable old man back there in spite of what he is and does."

"He wasn't always that way."

"I know. But the point is, Mandy, he's your father and you love him even though he doesn't treat you worth a damn."

"Pa doesn't treat anybody good. Not since Ma and my brother died."

"Maybe so, but that doesn't make taking his guff any easier. I respect the grit and courage you have shown lately in standing up to your father when you know it's necessary. Whether you realize it or not, your mind is now a lot sharper than his and it's up to you—not him—to make the right decisions for yourself and this herd. Bart has already lost one ranch, don't let him lose the one that's waiting for you in Montana."

"But how do you change it around?"

"Change what?"

Mandy frowned in the moonlight. "You know. All your life you look up to someone and listen to what they say. You obey them and then suddenly . . . you have to make all the big decisions and tell them what to do!"

"It isn't easy." The Gunsmith stared into the darkness. "But for what it's worth, Mandy, I couldn't handle it any better than you are. And that's a big part of why I respect you."

Her smile came slowly, but it grew wide and happy. "I believe that," she said, taking his hand and placing it on her breast. "And I also believe maybe it's time to stop talking and start making love."

He could not have agreed more. Clint stood up and hurriedly undressed watching Mandy as she did the same. When they were naked, he said, "Guess we had better spread out the old bedroll to keep out of any pricklies."

He picked his bedroll up and shook it hard. It cracked and the herd of cattle suddenly came awake. Clint didn't notice. He shook it once more with an exaggerated bit of flair and the cattle spooked. With horror, he saw them bolt and explode across the dark prairie.

"Oh no!" Mandy cried, grabbing her clothes as the entire herd thundered into the darkness. They heard Bart's startled shout of alarm as they yanked on their clothes and fought to get their feet back into their boots. Half dressed, stumbling toward their horses, Mandy and the Gunsmith tore across the camp.

"What the goddamn hell is going on?" Bart raged. "Where have you two been!"

"Later," Clint yelled, grabbing his saddle, pad, and bridle before dashing toward his horse. "We've got a stampede on our hands!"

Bart cussed a blue streak and by the time he was out of breath, Clint and Mandy were mounted and racing after their herd. The crossbreds were as fast as antelope and all Clint could see was the dust in their wake.

What a lousy way to spend the rest of the night!

What a waste of a day thinking about how he and Mandy were going to make love in the moonlight.

Goddamn stupid, spooky roan cattle!

Because of Duke's speed, Clint was soon a mile ahead of Mandy and yet it still took him another four miles to overtake the cattle. At least they were racing north in the proper direction. Clint overtook the slowest of the herd but even they were running with amazing swiftness. He had to really extend Duke to his fullest to overtake the leaders. When he reached them and was running nose to nose with them, he was not exactly sure what was required. He was reluctant to use his gun to try to turn them because this was Comanche country and a gunshot carried a long way on these Southern Plains.

Clint untied his lariat and thought about trying to rope what seemed to be the leader, but he was a lousy roper and so he tried to nudge in on the animal.

"Yahhhh!" he shouted, leaning in close to the beast and whacking the daylights out of it with his coiled rope.

The bull was huge and definitely not pleased. It hooked at Duke's shoulder and the wicked tip of his three-foot-long horn sliced hair and hide. Duke grunted and veered away so sharply he almost unseated the Gunsmith.

Clint saw the glistening blood on Duke's shoulder and it filled him with boiling fury. "Damn you!" he bellowed at the racing bull. "I ought to put a slug in your demented brain and be done with this!"

The bull seemed not to care or perhaps it realized that Clint would not risk a gunshot and was bluffing. In either event, it was reaching for ground and had steadily pulled away from the herd which followed with blind devotion. Its eyes were rolling around and around like a shaking jar of white and black marbles. It looked plumb loco to Clint and he stayed far enough away from it to keep those damned dagger-horns from ripping at Duke again.

Clint uncoiled his lariat and fashioned a loop. It was not easy on a racing horse but he managed. He whirled the loop around and around and then he edged Duke in so close that he could almost drop the loop over the animal's sweeping set of horns. The bull tried to hook at Duke again but the horse was ready this time and easily dodged the parry.

"Gotcha!" Clint shouted as he tightened the loop and dallied the end around his saddlehorn. He pulled gently on the reins and Duke slowed, but when the bull hit the end of the rope, it almost tore Duke out of his iron shoes.

Amazingly, the huge bull was every bit as strong and determined to run as Duke was in trying to stop it.

"The hell with this!" Clint shouted angrily as he remembered seeing what an old vaquero had done in a similar situation. Clint reined Duke hard in behind the bull. It was too dark and he was too inexperienced yet to know if what he wanted to do was going to work. But he felt the rope go slack for an instant and then, as it snapped like a whip across the bull's flying hocks, it jerked the legs out from under the beast and Clint saw the bull do a complete somersault.

"Yeeehaw!" he shouted as the huge roan bull crashed to the earth and plowed across about sixty feet of dirt and grass.

The bull was stunned. It lay moaning with its tongue hanging out of the side of its face. The rest of the herd braked to a sliding stop beside their fallen leader. Huffing and puffing like a bunch of miniature steam engines, they stared dumbly at the bull until it began to show signs of life.

A cow grew disinterested and started eating grass. Another followed her example and Clint dismounted and nervously untied his rope from the bull's massive horns. He walked back to Duke coiling his rope and almost feeling like he could make a real cowhand if it came right down to being necessary.

Clint examined Duke's bloodied shoulder. "I'll put some grease on it. Might leave a little white scar across the black but I doubt it."

Duke nickered softly as Clint affectionately scratched his horse behind the ears. The herd was settling down real fast. But they sure could run!

Mandy reached Clint just as he swung back into the saddle.

"What happened?"

Clint tied his lariat to his saddle. "I roped the bull leader and stopped him. The rest sort of decided the fun was over."

"You roped a stampeding bull!" It was clear she was having trouble believing this story. Clint had made no pretense of trying to be something he was not and he had told her that he wasn't much of a roper.

"That's right."

Mandy pulled off her battered Stetson and smiled. "Is that him?"

She was pointing to the only animal that was down.

"Yep."

"Did you break his neck?"

Clint's smile evaporated. "I don't think so."

Mandy untied her own rope. She was good with one and she could use it like a whip well enough to nail a fly at twenty feet. She popped the bull twice on his bulging testicles, hard and fast. The bull bawled pathetically but it scrambled to its feet.

"You didn't break its neck," she said with a sigh of relief.

"I guess not."

"Its a good thing. That's Old General Sherman, my pa's favorite of the herd. You kill him, he tries to kill you."

"He may anyway," Clint said, remembering how his ignorance in flapping his bedroll had started this whole thing in the first place.

"No he won't," Mandy said. "Because I'll stand beside you and conjure up some story to cover what really happened."

"You'd lie to your father?"

"Damn right," Mandy said with real conviction.

Clint nodded. Mandy was pretty, courageous, and also very, very bright.

EIGHTEEN

They skirted the Mescalero Plains and finally reached the Canadian River as they moved doggedly on to climb into the higher, greener hills and mountains.

"I think we are about in Colorado, now," Clint said as they crossed over Raton Pass and stared out at a land that undulated gently downward all the way to Pueblo, Colorado. To their left, the distant Sangre de Christo Mountains were still mantled with snow and stood majestic in the distance.

"Colorado is beautiful," Mandy said with admiration.

"But it'll never be Texas," Bart groused. "Never in a hundred damn years."

Clint suppressed a smile. Since the night of the stampede, he and Bart had finally reached some unspoken understanding. Maybe Bart finally realized that his daughter was a grown woman and had a right to make her own decisions about who she loved and made love to. At any rate, he and Mandy often walked off after dark to find a secluded place to be together. The old man might not like it, but he also seemed to realize that he could not change it.

"Clint, have you ever been to Montana?" Mandy asked.

"A time or two."

"What's it like?"

"It's mighty big and pretty country."

Bart grumped. "Not as big as Texas!"

Clint nodded. "That's true enough. But Montana is sure enough good cattle country. Most all of it."

"But the winters," Mandy said with a note of concern in her voice. "I've heard they are terrible."

Clint would have liked to have been more reassuring, but that would not have been right. "Yes," he conceded. "The winters are tough. They get blizzards and . . ."

"You ever heard of a Texas norther?" Bart asked. "These cattle of mine can weather a blizzard better than a goddamn polar penguin! Why, they love the cold and they'll get fat on nothing but icicles."

"Icicles?"

"That's right!"

"Pa, come on now, tell the truth."

Bart almost grinned. "Well, fact is, these cattle do get along pretty good in cold weather. Better than anything except maybe buffalo."

"They'll have their test, all right," Clint said. "But I'm sure they will be fine. And if they winter well, you'll have Montana, Wyoming, and Dakota ranchers begging for breeding stock."

Bart grinned. "Hear that, girl?"

"I heard."

Four days later as they neared Pueblo, Colorado, they were met by three men wearing badges. Clint relaxed. "It's the law and no need for worry."

But Bart did not agree. "Whenever I see a badge, I always worry. You never know what some of these tin-starred bastards have on their minds.

"Lawmen seem to think that they can run everybody's lives but their own. I don't like this."

"Howdy!" Clint said with a smile as the three men drew in their horses. "Nice day, isn't it?"

The three men stared at the herd. The one in the middle, a big man with a round, red face and deep-set black eyes, spat tobacco juice and said, "You're Texans."

It wasn't a question and, somehow, it held a note of

contempt that made the smile on Clint's lips fade. "We are coming from Texas."

"I'm a goddamn Texan!" Bart growled. "What business is it of yours?"

"Those are Texas cattle, aren't they?"

"So what?" Mandy asked. "There any law against bringing Texas cattle through Colorado?"

"There sure as hell is, ma'am," the leader said as he again spat tobacco. "You see, a couple of months ago, some Texans brought infected cattle through this country and our herds caught your plague."

"Our cattle are clean and healthy!" Bart shouted. "So get the hell out of our way!"

The leader reached for his pistol but Clint had him covered in the blink of an eyelash. "I think," the Gunsmith said quietly, "that you and your friends had best believe this little herd of prize cattle is all right. We mean no trouble, but we won't be ramrodded, either."

The red-faced man was all puffed up with anger and his two friends were grim and dangerous-looking. "You got two choices," the leader said tightly, "you can turn those cattle the hell around and get across the New Mexico line and out of our jurisdiction, or you can come on ahead and we'll quarantine the herd."

"For how long?" Clint asked.

"Six months."

Both Bart and his daughter shouted. "No!"

The leader of the Colorado riders said, "I give you three fair warning. We are legally deputized to use whatever force is required to carry out our duties."

Bart pulled out his gun. "Let's kill the bastards and be done with this nonsense."

"Pa, don't!"

Clint nodded. "She's right, Bart. The way it stands right now, we have a problem that might be solvable. If we kill them, we will be tracked down and hung by the law."

"You gonna put that gun away and turn back, or what!"

Clint looked to Mandy and her father. "They're your cattle."

Mandy said, "We're going to skirt Pueblo and, if necessary, your entire county. But we are coming through, mister."

"Then you'll face arrest or worse."

"Get the hell outa here before I gun you all down!" Bart raged.

The three range detectives wheeled their horses around as the leader yelled, "You'll live to regret this, all of you!"

They raced away to the north. Clint, Mandy, and Bart watched them until they disappeared over a ridge.

"We may have a problem," Clint said.

"I should have killed them," Bart muttered. "Could have buried them so they'd never be found."

But Mandy shook her head. "We go on and we face whatever they have waiting. But we circle to the east. If they come after us, it'll be on their heads, not ours."

Clint agreed. There was a chance that these three men were exceeding their actual authority and hoping to extort some money to fill their pockets. But that wasn't likely. Either way, they had come much too far to turn back for Texas now.

NINETEEN

Their mood was grim as they pushed the crossbred cattle northeast. Mandy had never seen this country, and Bart didn't act like he had, either—or perhaps he just did not remember it. That left the responsibility up to the Gunsmith and he decided to roughly follow the Huerfano River until it joined with the Arkansas. That would bring them about twenty miles east of Pueblo and maybe any trouble that awaited.

"But if they have their minds set on stopping this herd, then they sure won't have any trouble catching us," Clint warned.

"If they come looking for trouble, we'll give them all they want," Mandy replied.

Clint looked off to the flank where Bart was riding alone. "You sound almost like your father."

"Thank you. In many ways, I take that as a compliment. My father has never been crowded or bullied and neither will I. As you know, there are times when being reasonable with people doesn't work. That's when you have to fight."

Clint frowned. "I agree. But getting yourself killed for nothing is foolish. If these men are telling the truth, they'll return with a dozen ranchers up in arms in addition to the sheriff and maybe even a couple of heavily armed deputies. I've faced long odds and won, but I don't make a habit of going up against impossible odds."

"So what are you suggesting?"

"I don't know yet," the Gunsmith replied slowly. "But I have nothing to prove to anyone by dying a fool. I'd like to think we can outsmart our enemies when we can't outgun them."

Mandy did not seem impressed. "If they come," she said, "and they want a fight, I don't care how many there are, we'll fight!"

Clint thought about that a lot during he next few days and nights. How did you tell someone as hardheaded and as proud as Bart and Mandy Roe that, every once in a while, you had to back off a little and come at the obstacles in your path from a different direction? You just could not try and run over everybody or everything in your path. You might get lucky and get away with it for a while, but sooner or later, you were going to either get broken or killed. The simple fact of the matter was, a man could be brave *and* smart, tough *and* smart.

Each morning they were on the trail before the sun was up. Clint had ridden quietly into Trinidad and bought more supplies and now they were well provisioned enough to reach Wyoming without stopping. All during this trail drive, he had insisted that he, not Bart, ride into a town and do the buying. Had Bart gone, the old man would have surely spent all their food money on whiskey. He'd probably also have gotten drunk, insulted anyone who wasn't a Texan and a cowman, and either gotten himself shot or hung.

On the third night after their warning, the crossbreds bolted off their bedground and stampeded eastward for almost ten miles before they could be turned and circled. The cattle were being pushed too hard and they were getting cantankerous and edgy.

"We need to slow them down," Bart complained. "They ain't getting enough time to graze. They're losing too much damned weight!"

Clint knew the man was right, but he was hoping, if they could just get north of Pueblo, maybe the range detectives

TRAIL DRIVE TO MONTANA 105

would decide it was not worth the trouble.

But even as he nurtured that hope, he knew that it was a poor one. And when they did come to the Arkansas River late one afternoon, there were at least twenty mounted and heavily armed law and cattlemen waiting to take custody of the herd.

Clint drew rein and heard the sound of two Winchesters being cocked for action. "That isn't the way to handle this," he warned. "What do we accomplish by dying and letting those men keep your cattle?"

"They can't keep them if they're shot dead," Bart reasoned.

"Well, neither can we. Mandy, you and your pa hold the herd to this side of the river. I'll ford it and go over to have a pow-wow with them. Maybe I can talk them into being a little more reasonable."

"You can try. But, Clint, they don't look one bit reasonable to me. You be careful. If anything . . ."

Clint said, "I'll be careful. Just give me a little time to talk. I can be pretty persuasive when I have to be."

"I know," she told him. "Boy, do I know."

Clint caught her meaning but said nothing more. What talking he needed to do was with the leader of the men facing him across the wide Arkansas River.

He put Duke into the water and the gelding took to it like he'd been raised by a flock of mallard ducks. When they emerged on the other side, Clint saw one of the men detach himself from the others and ride forward a few paces.

"Well, goddamn!" the sheriff said with a low whistle, "if it ain't the famous Gunsmith!"

Clint could not place the sheriff who rode forward. The man was riding a buckskin mare. He was tall, brown-haired, and in his thirties. He had a handsome face that was starting to get too beefy and his belly was straining at the shirt buttons. Ten years ago he had obviously been a lady-killer, ten years from now he would be too fat to ride a horse.

"Howdy, Sheriff!"

"You remember me!" The man grinned hugely and stuck out a plump but very powerful hand. "Name is Ace Varga. I met you once up in Jerome, Arizona. Saw you kill Monty Reid, John Beers and Rattlesnake Red all at once. Best damn gunfight I ever saw."

"I remember the fight," Clint said. "But I don't quite remember what you . . ."

"I was the goddamn sheriff! You took on those three before I could even get out of my office."

Now Clint remembered. Remembered how he had sent word asking for Ace Varga to apprehend the trio before they carried out their threat to kill him on sight. Later, Ace had insisted that he had never gotten the message but Clint had requestioned the boy and knew that the sheriff of Jerome had been lying through his teeth.

Clint concealed his true feelings. "Well, Sheriff," he said, forcing a friendliness that he did not feel. "We seem to have a little problem here. Those few cows, steers, calves, and bulls we have are as healthy as we are. And, like we told the man there," Clint jerked a thumb in the direction of the leader of the range detectives, "all we want to do is pass on by. We've even gone a considerable distance out of our way to stay clear of Pueblo and any Colorado cattle."

The sheriff's smile tightened. "We do appreciate that and are sorry for the trouble. But you see, Gunsmith, this county appointed me the law and they got a law on the books right now that says all Texas cattle passing through southern Colorado have to be quarantined for six months."

"That's unreasonable. It'll be winter in six months and we'd never get this herd all the way to the Yellowstone River before the snows."

The sheriff shrugged with exaggerated sympathy. "Listen, after the quarantine, some of our local ranchers will take them off your hands. Can't pay top dollar, but they'll pay something. Won't you, boys?"

The men were listening. Several of the older ones nodded. Clint smelled a rat. It suddenly occurred to him that this

TRAIL DRIVE TO MONTANA 107

was an ideal way for these ranchers to get damn cheap cattle. Faced with the prospect of selling now or hanging on and feeding a herd for six months, anyone would be forced to sell.

Clint leaned on his saddlehorn. "Ace," he said, softly so that his words could not be overheard, "why don't we strike a little deal here? There must be some way we can avoid me putting a bullet through your brisket and then getting myself killed by your friends."

Sheriff Ace Varga's mouth dropped and he swallowed as the implication struck home. "Listen, Gunsmith, you're up against a loaded deck here."

"And you're up against a fast gun that's going to kill you first if you don't figure us a way out of this mess."

Varga nervously licked his lips. "We can't work nothing out here. It'll have to be in town. Can you bring the herd to the outskirts of Pueblo?"

"I could ask them to do that. That is Mandy and Bart Roe and they own the cattle, not me. Bart is a hard man and it'll take some talking."

"Then swim back and talk your ass off, Gunsmith. I sure don't want no gun trouble between us."

"I imagine not," Clint said. "Because you know your next stop would be boot hill."

Varga flushed with anger but most of it was show. "I gotta take you in for a talk," he said stubbornly. He glanced back at the eleven men who waited. "You can see how this thing is."

"I can see just fine," Clint said.

He swam Duke back across the river, and when he told Bart and Mandy what had been proposed, they both looked a little relieved. "So we work something out," Clint said.

"Fine," Bart answered. "But I won't stand for blackmail. They want a veterinarian or doctor to check our cattle before we ride on, that is all right. Anything more, tell 'em to shove it."

Clint figured that they would want more but there was

no sense in telling that to Bart or Mandy right now. In a situation like this, you just took things one step at a time. With a little luck, a little diplomacy, and a lot of hard bargaining, maybe a peace could be struck and a deal made.

Someone had to give somewhere.

TWENTY

Clint did not like the idea of having to strike some kind of a deal with Ace Varga. He might do it, but the thought of fattening this man's wallet with some under-the-table arrangement did not sit well at all. There were crooked lawman, Clint had met a few in his travels, but they were a rarity. Mostly, lawmen were overworked, underpaid individuals with an abundance of character and more than their share of courage. That was why, when the Gunsmith came across a man like Ace Varga, he boiled with anger.

"So," Ace was saying as they rode into Pueblo, "I sort of got tired of throwing drunk miners in the caboose every night and left Jerome, Arizona, while I still had my front teeth in my face. All those men wanted to do was visit the whorehouses, drink bad whiskey, and fight. I never seen men to match them. Most was from Europe, especially Wales. Those Welshmen, now they aren't big, but they are tough and they fight if you even look at them cross-eyed. Here, it's a lot different."

"I'll bet," Clint said cryptically.

"Nice, clean, quiet cattle town here. I keep the bad element out of Pueblo. Put them on stages and send them to Leadville or up to Denver. If you don't let the riffraff stay around, you don't have big problems. 'Course, you know that, Gunsmith. Hell, you wrote the book on town taming."

Clint said nothing. Pueblo was a nice community. Trees lined the wide streets, the houses looked painted and the lawns well tended. There were flower gardens and the main street of business was a definite cut above most western towns of similar size.

"Mostly, Gunsmith, this is a cattle-raising town. A little gold and silver mining, but not much. Some commerce and freighting, but mostly farms and ranches. Well, here's my office building. Not bad, huh?"

It was obvious that Ace took pride in his office and well that he should. It was an imposing, two-story brick building. Downstairs a big window gave a full view of the street and Clint guessed that the cells were upstairs because that's where the windows were barred.

"It's nice," he said, looking at the big, hand-carved and lettered, "Sheriff's Office" sign with Ace Varga's name in bold relief. "Real nice." What Clint was wondering was how a town this size managed to pay and support such a huge jail and sheriff's office.

"Well," the sheriff said, as a deputy opened the door and came out to study Clint as if he were a botanical specimen. "I told these people that I was tired of working for cowboys' wages and laying my life on the line every single day. They had problems and they were desperate. The last three sheriffs had been either murdered, or run out of town, so I could write my own ticket. They pay me a hundred dollars a month and the salary of one damned good deputy. Latigo Raines is might fast with a six-gun. Might even equal your own speed, Gunsmith."

"Latigo, this here is the Gunsmith. I guess you have heard all about him, same as everyone else. I've even told you the story about what happened in Jerome."

"A bunch of times," Latigo said without a smile. He sized Clint up and down. "I thought you'd be a bigger man."

Clint smiled coldly at the lean, hawk-faced young man before him. "I'm big enough, and so is my gun."

Latigio stiffened as if he had been slapped. His eyes narrowed and, if he were a rattlesnake, Clint would have figured him ready to strike.

"You boys might as well go about your business for a while," the sheriff said to the riders who had accompanied them on the long ride.

"We'll talk to you as soon as you're through with him," one of them said in a voice that carried more than the hint of a threat. "You don't let us down, now."

Ace nodded and tried to look relaxed. He failed completely. "Sure. Sure. You men go on over and have a drink. I'll be along directly."

Clint turned his back on all of them because he did not like the way this deal was shaping up. He walked Duke over to a water trough and let the animal drink. When the horse was finished, he tied him to a hitching rail and followed the sheriff and his deputy inside.

"What do you think?" Ace Varga asked, with a sweep of his hand to include the entire room. "Like it?"

Clint nodded. "Looks more like a mayor's office than the sheriff's."

Ace liked that. He laughed loudly. "Sit down and make yourself comfortable, Gunsmith. We got some talking to do. Latigo, why don't you go make the rounds and keep your ear to the floor. I want to know what is up. Savvy?"

Latigo nodded but he did not look happy to go. When he was gone, the sheriff eased his bulk into a new swivel chair and carefully placed his boots on his polished desk while Clint looked around.

The place was too damned clean and orderly for Clint's liking. A good, hard-working sheriff ought to have nothing but old, scarred furniture that was too damned sorry-looking for anyone else to use. He ought to have Wanted posters tacked all over the walls and he needed to glance at them each and every day just in case one of the wanted outlaws rode through his town. Hell, this office really did look like it should belong to the mayor. There were framed pictures on the wall and every damned thing!

"Like a drink of good whiskey?" Ace Varga asked with a wink.

"No thanks. Maybe later. Let's talk." Clint wanted to settle this matter and get back to Mandy and her father before they got edgy.

Ace put his feet back to the floor and leaned forward in his chair. "I'll come right to the point, Gunsmith. We want those cattle quarantined, and then we want to buy them cheap."

"That's what I expected." Clint smiled coldly. "But that won't happen. You see, Ace, these are very special cattle. Crossbred cattle that you or these ranchers have never seen the equal of. They are the best bred cattle in the country and each one of them is worth plenty."

"That's even better! Why, we can get 'em for a song and then sell them at the Denver livestock show that is coming up in the next couple of weeks! We can make a killing."

"Afraid not. Those roan cattle belong to the Roes, Mandy and her father Bart."

"That's Bart Roe? I heard of him. But, Jesus, he looks bad! What happened to all his hair?"

"That's a long story. But he's also old and he drinks too much. His health isn't too good and his eyes are failing. Despite all that, he can still fight and he won't sell. Not for anything."

Ace begin to shake his head. "You don't understand, Gunsmith. He won't have any choice. You see, we quarantine the herd and charge him two bits a day per animal for feed and keeping. In just one lousy week, he'll owe us nearly a hundred dollars! I'll bet he hasn't even got that much. I tell you, he has to sell! And you'll get part of whatever the profits are after we sell them in Denver."

Clint had heard all that he needed to hear. He rose to his feet and said, "Now hear this the first time because it's the last time I'm going to say it. Those people are my friends and you're not going to cheat them this way."

Ace swallowed. "It's the young girl, ain't it? You're screwin' her and that's . . ."

TRAIL DRIVE TO MONTANA

The man never finished. The back of Clint's hand struck him in the face and knocked him and his fancy swivel chair over backward. Ace let out an enraged bellow, and when his head struck the polished floor, he cursed and clawed for his gun. He must have been dazed to do such a stupid thing because Clint had his own gun out of his holster and pointed right between the man's eyes.

"Freeze, Ace, or I'll put you out of your misery."

Ace froze. Hatred burned in his face for an instant but then he looked past Clint and he actually smiled. "You freeze, Gunsmith, or Latigo is going to blow a big hole through your chest."

Clint stiffened. "You're bluffing."

"No he's not," Latigo said with a happy whisper. "Now do as the sheriff says or I'll have the pleasure of smattering you all over these nice walls with this big old shotgun."

Clint took a deep breath and let it out slowly. Latigo had sneaked in from a back door so it was clear this had been a set-up all the way if Clint refused to deal into their game. He dropped his gun.

"Damn," Latigo whispered, "I sure was hoping you would give me an excuse to blow you apart."

"Sorry about that."

The sheriff collected the fallen Colt .45 and said, "Gunsmith, I'm sorry you weren't smart enough to cut yourself into this little arrangement. But you made your choice and now you have to pay the consequences. Latigo, nice work. Now take him upstairs and lock him up tight."

"You won't get away with this," Clint growled as Latigo shoved the shotgun into his spine, prodding him toward the stairs.

"Yes we will," Ace said. "How do you think that the town leaders pay for all this and our salaries? The townspeople would sure never allow it. So the money comes out our cattle profits. No one in Pueblo has any idea of how the deal works and we keep it just that way. Right, Latigo?"

"Right," the man said. "And no one ever will."

Clint spun around and headed upstairs. He was shoved into one of the finest cells he had ever seen. The walls and floor were set solidly with brick and mortar. The bars were new and the locks were Swiss-made and tamper-proof. He wasn't going to escape.

Clint moved over to the window and stared down into the street to see Ace swaggering toward the saloon. There was a whistle on his lips and Clint gripped the heavy iron bars until his knuckles grew white.

Dammit, he raged inwardly, what in the hell was going to become of Mandy and old Bart now!

TWENTY-ONE

Mandy awoke in the night reaching for her gun. She clenched it in her fist and stared out into darkness until the bullfrogs began to croak again along the marshy banks of the Arkansas River. She put the gun away and closed her eyes, listening to the comforting hoot of an owl and crickets chirping.

It was very difficult not having Clint Adams beside her. With him close, Mandy felt safe. Today, her father had ridden off to find a ranch house late in the afternoon and had returned long after midnight, drunk as a lord. Mandy had pretended to be asleep while he had cussed and reeled around the camp, angry because he could not find his nightshirt. After a while, he had gone to bed fully dressed and, now, she could see his dim outline and hear his measured breathing. It was funny, when he was really drunk, like tonight, his snoring was not nearly so loud as usual.

She drifted off to sleep thinking about Clint and wondering what would happen to him when she and her father finally managed to reach Montana. Deep down, she guessed that she knew the Gunsmith would move on and leave her. He had let her know that he was not a marrying kind of a man and that he was restless. Yes, she thought, he had told her that in so many ways. And sometimes, during the long, dry New Mexico miles, she had sensed a deep need inside him to be released from his self-imposed responsibility for her welfare. Quite often, seeing his restlessness, she had almost ordered him to leave her—but her good intentions exceeded her will and her strength. She needed Clint Adams; without the famous Gunsmith, Mandy believed she would have no chance whatsoever of getting this herd to Montana.

Mandy finally slept—deeply, until she awoke with a start hearing her father's shouted warning in the faint, predawn gray light. She cried, "What's wrong . . . Pa, where are you?"

She saw his dim outline and when he fired his gun, she could see the muzzle-flash reach out like a flaming finger of death. She followed its direction and that was when she realized that rustlers were stealing her herd.

Mandy dropped back to her bedroll and wildly groped for her gun. She heard her father cursing the cattle rustlers and firing. Suddenly, a rider out in the darkness cried out in pain and then the cattle rustlers turned their attention to Bart. A half dozen guns breathed fire and death.

"Pa, no!" Mandy cried as she heard the sickening impact of bullets punching into her father's body.

She came up with her own gun, but he reeled around and tore it from her fingers, groaning, "The river, Mandy, your only chance is the river!"

The riders were coming. She could hear the thunder of their horses' hooves and feel her pa pushing her backward toward the steep riverbank.

Mandy tried to fight her way around him but he grabbed her arm and cried, "Please, girl, for me. I want you to . . . ahh, to live!"

She felt and heard two more bullets strike his body and then, as she cried out in rage and helpless anger, he dropped her gun and used his last surge of life to throw her bodily into the current.

Mandy sank deep into the swirling water. It was cold and it snatched her breath away. She struck a submerged log and the air was pounded from her lungs. For a terrifying moment, she was caught in the slick, mossy branches and then she tore herself free. After what seemed an eternity, she finally clawed her way back to the black surface and sucked in the life-giving oxygen. The night was silent except for the sound of the river. It seemed to Mandy that she must surely be the only living person in Colorado.

Mandy struggled toward shore. She reached it easily enough, for Bart had taught her to swim powerfully in the muddy Rio Grande River. She started to climb out of the water but the riverbank was slick and she fell.

Two rifles barked out and Mandy felt a slug burn the flesh of her lower arm. She stifled a cry and threw herself back into the water as men shouted to find and kill her.

Mandy relaxed. She let the river take ahold of her, mind and body. She allowed the soft water to tug and massage, twist and carry her away from the herd and the death. Bart was finished. She knew he had given his last bit of strength to save her life.

And that he had, despite all his meanness, loved her after all.

I'll live, Mandy thought. I'll find a way to hide from them and I'll find some way to get my cattle back!

She looked up at the dying stars. "You won't have died for nothing, Pa. I swear that to you on the last star in heaven!"

Daylight found her eleven miles below her camp and digging under a steep bank where muskrats had lived for generations. The river had cut back the bank at least four feet and the muskrats had expanded that. Mandy, shivering and covered with mud, found a hiding place where only her head was uncovered far under the bank.

There, she remained for untold hours until her shivering became so violent that she could no longer keep her teeth from chattering. Besides, her strength was quickly being eroded by the cold water and she could not stand the dripping, slick mud she felt would collapse any moment on her.

But when she eased out toward the sunlight, she heard voices calling back and forth and she knew that they were close and coming closer.

"Damn you!" she whispered, gritting her teeth and moving back under the bank. "Damn you anyway!"

She would wait a little longer. Maybe even until nightfall if she could hold out that long. And then what?

Mandy wasn't sure. All she knew for certain was that the cattle were gone, Clint was gone, and her father was dead. They would bury her father's body in an unmarked grave where it would never be found.

Hanging onto the slippery root of a tree, Mandy began to cry for Bart, and when her sobbing became too loud, she buried her face in the water. But the leaden coldness that seeped into her bones could not begin to touch the fire in her heart that burned for revenge over those who had done this terrible thing.

TWENTY-TWO

The pretty young shill that worked at Pueblo's Red Rose Saloon lay still on the bed, feeling her right eye swelling shut and tasting blood in her mouth. Claire wondered if Latigo Raines had split her eyebrow open or if his fist had just left her with a real shiner.

The bedside lamp was on and she opened her left eye just a crack and saw him getting dressed. She wished she had a knife, she would drive its blade deep into his back and be finished with him forever.

No I wouldn't, she thought miserably. I haven't the guts to face either prison or a hangman. So, if he won't let me leave town and he keeps beating me, how do I escape from this mess before he kills me some night in a fit of jealousy?

"Claire?"

She closed her good eye and feigned sleep.

He touched her shoulder. "Hey, Claire! I said I was sorry. I lost my temper again, but I just get so goddamn mad thinking about you and how you're here all the time with other men. What they do to you."

The very same thing you do to me, only you expect it for free! she raged silently.

"Claire, I'm sorry about your face. If you need to go see a doctor, maybe I can get you a couple a bucks next payday. But you gotta understand that I won't stand no sass from my woman!"

When she did not answer, Latigo ripped the blanket aside

and grabbed her heavy breast and squeezed it. "Don't you play dead on me, goddamn you!"

The pain was so excruciating that Claire almost passed out. A scream built in her throat but he saw it coming and clamped his hand over her mouth.

"Don't you scream, goddamn you, or I'll really bust your face up good!"

She was so afraid she wet the bed. Shame, fear, and the intense pain made tears leak from the corners of her eyes. I won't scream, she breathed. "Please, Latigo, you're hurting me!"

He laughed. Bent down and took her breast into his mouth, then bit her nipple hard. Claire couldn't help it. She did scream and her fingernails clawed at his face. She felt them cut into his cheeks and he yelled. Then, he doubled up his fist and punched her. Almost gratefully, Claire lost consciousness.

Two nights later, she could move, think, and see well enough to decide that she had to get away from Pueblo before Latigo killed her. No one in town would dare to help her except the Gunsmith.

Claire remembered everything that Latigo had said about the man and how jealousy and hatred had driven the deputy into something close to a killing frenzy.

The Gunsmith. A man who would not be afraid. A man who would help her escape and be able to protect her from Latigo's deadly gun.

Claire took the Colt revolver and made sure it was unloaded. Then, she sat down and wrote the Gunsmith a long letter telling him exactly what she could do to help him escape and what he must do for her.

She was not accustomed to writing, and it was past midnight before she finished. She left the message unsigned. She sealed it in an envelope and stuffed it inside one of her snagged and oldest pair of silk stockings. She also put six bullets in with the letter before tying it all up neatly and then attaching it to a long piece of twine.

Claire's room was on the second floor, just three buildings down from the sheriff's office. And though there were two gaps of about eight feet between the buildings whose rooftops she would have to traverse, she did not think it would be too difficult. She was strong and young. As a girl, she had jumped streams much wider without ever getting her feet wet. And if she failed and plunged to her death, then so what? Sooner or later, Latigo would surely beat her brains out anyway. To Claire's mind, she had absolutely nothing to lose and everything to gain by trying.

She waited until there was no one in the hallway and then she ducked out of her room and hurried up to the stairway leading to the roof. Her heart was thumping wildly but it was because of excitement, not fear.

The Gunsmith awoke hearing the faint brushing of something against the window bars of his cell. At first, he thought he was dreaming but when the sound grew more insistent, he opened his eyes and then moved over to the window.

The silk stocking was dangling inches from the window. He tried to reach his hand through but it was impossible. The gap between the bars was less than two inches wide and he could not quite get his hand through the narrow space. He looked up but could see nothing.

"Closer," he whispered. "Swing it into the window."

Whoever was on top heard him because the stuffed stocking moved out, then came back in, twice. With a desperate grab, he captured its fabric by his fingertips and pulled the stocking through the bars. He untied the stocking and extracted the letter. Having read it twice, he nodded grimly and placed the bullets in his pocket, then scribbled, using the back of the same letter and a stubby pencil that the woman had included: "Give me a gun and I swear I will help you reach Denver."

He shoved the stocking back through the bars and waited anxiously. Would she believe him? She had nothing but his word that he would find her room and sneak her out of Pueblo on horseback tonight.

It seemed like an eternity before the sock returned. This time, the woman wasted no time but began to swing it in and out. It clanked noisily against the bars twice before Clint caught it and snaked it through.

'Thanks!'' he whispered out into the black night. "Get ready because I'll be there early in the morning."

"Thank you" came a faint, desperate voice. "Please don't fail!"

"I won't."

Clint held the gun up to the starlight. It was just a battered old Colt but it seemed to work fine. He checked out its action and saw that the trigger spring was much too tight. He pulled out a dime and managed to unfasten the handle screw and make the proper adjustment by feel because he was so familiar with this kind of weapon. Satisfied now that the gun was in proper working order, Clint carefully loaded the Colt and shoved it under his shirt.

He lay down on his bunk and waited for morning and breakfast to be brought up to him by Latigo Raines. Over and over he rehearsed how he must do this thing. If he killed Latigo without getting his hands on the keys, he was a dead man, for he would surely be hung by a lynch mob within the following hour.

I'll only have one chance, he thought, and I had better not fail.

TWENTY-THREE

Latigo came up the stairs, his footsteps much lighter than those of Sheriff Ace Varga. Clint slipped the Colt under his waistband right along his backbone.

"Morning, Deputy!"

The man looked at him through a pair of bloodshot and suspicious eyes. "What's good about it?" he demanded. "Especially for you. We're going to have to figure out a way to either shoot or hang you."

"Of course you would. You couldn't have me tell the entire town what has been going on here."

"You got that much right." Latigo dropped down on one knee. "Stay back, damn you!" he growled.

"Sure," Clint said, waiting until the man was off balance and then drawing the old Colt revolver from behind his back. "Now don't move and you might live through this!"

Latigo saw the gun and he started to draw his own. But on one knee, he had no chance and he must have known it instantly. He froze and Clint jumped forward and placed the gun at his forehead. "Now, real slow and easy, you give me those keys and I'll open the door myself."

With a hiss, Latigo yanked the precious keys from his pocket and, to Clint's horror, tossed them down at the stairway. Clint heard them striking the stairs all the way to the floor.

Latigo grinned wickedly. "Hand the gun to me, the game is over."

Clint cocked his gun. "If I die behind these bars, you are going to die in front of them. You move an inch and you're a dead man. I swear you are!"

Latigo saw a killing determination in the Gunsmith's face and he seemed to understand that they were at the point of a Mexican standoff. "The sheriff will be coming along sometime this morning. He'll see the keys down there on the floor and know something is wrong up here."

"Yeah," Clint breathed. "And that's going to be the moment of truth for all of us. Will Varga come up shooting, or will he unlock this cell and let me out in return for your life?"

"He don't give a damn about me! He might even hope you kill me."

"I can believe that."

Latigo began to sweat. "Listen," he said, "maybe I acted too fast. Maybe I did a stupid thing just now with the cell keys."

"I'm sure you did," Clint said. "So what do you suggest?"

"I . . . I don't know. You see, I have to go down and get those keys. But I'd come right back up and . . ."

Clint laughed in the younger man's face. "Don't insult me, Latigo. You'd get a shotgun and come up that staircase. You'd lay down on the stairs out of my line of fire, shove the shotgun over the top, and pull the trigger. I'd be meat and you'd never even have to risk your life. Uh-uh, Deputy. We'll wait until the sheriff arrives and I'll take my chances with him."

It was ten o'clock when they heard the downstairs door open and footsteps cross the polished hardwood floor to stop at the base of the stairs. When Clint heard the keys rattle, he said, "One word of warning and you are dead."

Now, Clint heard the stairs creaking softly as someone was obviously sneaking up them. He tensed, pressed the barrel of his gun against Latigo's head, and waited.

"Gunsmith?" a woman whispered. "Are you still alive?"

Relief flooded through Clint. "Come on up and let me out of here. Hurry!"

"Claire!" Latigo screamed, forgetting Clint and spinning around to leap at her. Clint had not expected that kind of crazed reaction, and now he had only one split second to decide what to do. There was no choice. If Latigo reached the girl, he would carry her down the stairs and kill her before coming back up to kill him.

Clint shot Latigo in the back of one knee. The deputy screamed. His momentum carried him into the girl and they tumbled and crashed down the stairs.

Clint grabbed the bars and shook them in helpless fury. He heard the woman cry in pain, then two tightly spaced gunshots followed. Clint yelled, "Come and get me, damn you, Latigo! Come on, crawl up these stairs with your shotgun!"

He heard moans and a crawling sound like a body dragging itself up each agonizing step. But, miraculously, the same woman reappeared.

Clint almost sank to his knees with gratitude. Her face was swollen and one eye was purplish, but he did not lie when he breathed, "You're the best-looking female I ever saw. Now pitch the keys over here and let me get you out of this town before they come and hang us both."

She nodded and weakly threw him the keys. Clint had the cell open in a second. He raced to the young woman's side and scooped her up in his arms.

"I won't desert you, honey. We go together or we don't go at all. Have you got the horses out back like you said?"

She laid her head on his shoulder, nodded, and began to cry. "I thought I would laugh if I could put a bullet through his heart. But . . . but I can't."

Clint took the stairs slowly and he had to step over the dead figure of Latigo Raines, who lay sprawled on the floor. Clint hurried across the room. He had the deputy's gun and the one this woman had dropped down from the roof to him. He would have liked to have grabbed a shotgun but when he peered out the window and saw that the street was empty and no one had heard the shots through the windows and heavy brick walls, he decided that a big shotgun would look too conspicuous.

"Here," he said, placing her in the sheriff's swivel chair and finding her a clean handkerchief in the sheriff's desk drawer, "dry your eyes. We have to walk out of here looking normal. You have to do that."

"Then I will," she managed to say. Her eyes started to drift toward the fallen deputy but Clint stepped into her line of sight. "Don't look at him. Just think about what he did to you and what he would have done if you hadn't killed him to save both our lives."

"All right." She shook her head as if to clear it. "My name is Claire," she said simply, as if it now took all of her concentration to remember.

Clint spotted his own gun and cartridge belt. He gave Claire her gun back, shoved Latigo's weapon into his pocket, and buckled his own gun on.

It felt good on his hip and he was ready. "Let's get the hell out of here," he said, taking the girl's arm and helping her up. "But remember, you have to look normal."

She straightened her back and raised her chin. "I can do that."

Clint took her arm and led her to the door. He opened it, looked both ways, and then they stepped out onto the boardwalk and started for the horses.

They were almost to the side alley they wanted when Ace Varga shouted, "Hey, stop! You're both under arrest!"

Clint grabbed Claire and they ran down the narrow alley toward the waiting horses. He threw the girl into her saddle and sprang onto Duke. Reining around, he started forward but the sheriff jumped into his path with his gun raised.

"Drop it," Clint shouted as he drew his own gun. "Drop it!"

Varga cursed and opened fire. His bullets were wild and too hurried. Clint drilled the man through his right shirt

TRAIL DRIVE TO MONTANA   127

pocket and Ace Varga was dead before they thundered past him in the alley. Moments later, they were out of town and racing north.

"Did you kill him?" Claire shouted as they rode stirrup to stirrup.

"Yes," the Gunsmith replied grimly.

"Good!"

Clint thought back to what he knew of Varga. How the man had used his badge to get wealthy off unfortunate cattlemen trying to drive their herds north. How he must have had to kill those very same cattlemen to keep the story from leaking out. How he might even have killed Mandy and her father to get the crossbreds.

"Yeah," Clint said through clenched teeth. "I guess it was at that."

TWENTY-FOUR

They raced along the riverbank with the morning light shining over a flat plain that reached clear across Kansas. It was a frosty morning, one with the promise of a late summer thunderstorm. Along the banks of the river, the trees were just beginning to change color as gold edged into their leaves.

Fall was coming and very soon after, in this hard, high country, would come winter. Clint could not help but feel a sense of urgency along with dread and worry. Where were Mandy and those crossbred cattle?

He halted at their first Arkansas River bedground. In moments, Clint read the sign of the attack and the victory of the cattle rustlers.

Clint swallowed with bitterness. He stood beside Duke, and his eyes scanned the battleground with a practiced eye.

"What's wrong?" Claire asked too loudly. "What are we stopping here for?"

Clint did not immediately answer. He moved right up the riverbank and studied the footprints. He found spent cartridges and saw where something had fallen and crushed the grass. Clint knelt and ran his fingers over the grass and found dried blood.

"I got a right to know what you are looking for," Claire said with rising impatience, her eyes constantly searching back toward Pueblo. "We are wasting time here. There must be a possee coming after us right now!"

Clint stared at the dark, swirling river. He wasn't sure that he trusted himself to speak. "There might be pursuit, but I doubt it. You see, both the sheriff and Latigo were in on a rustling scheme and murder. That's why I'd never have been allowed to go to trial. They could never let me talk."

The girl blinked. Comprehension flooded her expression and she grinned broadly. "You mean that Latigo and Ace Varga were the only two who knew the real reason you were even in that jail?"

"Not exactly. The men who took me into town and are involved with the cattle rustling also knew. But they'd never have said anything."

"Then . . . then we are free?" She could not believe it.

"I think so," Clint said. "Oh, the town will be all astir over the killing of their deputy and sheriff, but when they start asking questions about who did it, no one will speak up."

"Jesus," Claire whispered. "This is too good to believe. But what are we doing here?"

Clint took a few minutes to tell her about Mandy and old Bart. About the small herd of crossbred cattle and how Ace Varga had used the threat of a quarantine to force cattlemen to practically give their herds away free to a handful of local cutthroat ranchers.

Throughout the explanation, Claire remained silent but her earlier smile had been replaced by a grim look. "They are both dead. Have to be. Varga was no fool. They would never allow witnesses."

"I know that," Clint said. "But you had to know Mandy and her father. They'd be very tough to kill."

"But at two against what . . . ten or fifteen?" Claire shook her head. "Gunsmith, you're grasping at a straw. They're for certain dead. The only possible chance they might have had is if they . . ."

Clint had his own theory, but he also wanted to hear Claire's. "If they what?

"If they dove into that river and swam to safety. Maybe

hid in the willows or tules farther down."

"That's right," Clint said, looking at her with new respect. "That's exactly what I was thinking. They would have been surprised at night and had no time to run. Hell, they would not have run no matter what the odds. Mandy told me that, but she needn't have. No, they'd have fought until it was obvious that they had no chance. Then, Mandy would have taken to the river."

"So we follow the river?"

"Yeah," Clint said, swinging up onto his horse. "We follow this river all the way to Kansas if we have to."

But the girl shook her head. "I can't do that," she said. "I have some friends in Denver. That's where I'm going from here."

Clint was almost relieved. Claire had taken a bad beating and was in no condition to go on a long, hard hunt. Her face was still swollen and she had badly twisted her knee when she and Latigo had tumbled down the stairs. It was best that she did not come along. "Sure. Will you be all right?"

"How about giving me my gun back?"

Clint nodded and gave her the old Colt she had slipped to him in the second-story jail cell. He was sad to see her leave. She had saved his live and even though she'd done it out of a need to save her own, it was still the result that counted. "I have some extra money," Clint said.

"Uh-uh," Claire replied. "I can make money anytime I want. But I don't need to do that anymore. I learned something back in Pueblo. If a girl is a whore, she gets treated like a whore. It's a one-way street to hell, and I'm stepping off that street and going in another direction. I got a sister in Denver that owns a café. No big thing, but she'll give me work until I find something better."

"I'm real glad to hear that," Clint said with real sincerity. "What's the name of that café? I'll stop when I come through."

"The Red Onion. Good food, honest prices."

Clint reached out and took Claire's hand. "I won't forget you," he said. "And I'll come by for a dinner before long."

"You'll get the best I can give you, Gunsmith. Anytime, anyplace, and for free. And I don't mean just food, either."

He grinned. "I thought you said you were through with that sort of thing."

"I am. No more spreading my legs for anyone who has a few lousy dollars. That's over with. From now on, I'll only make love with men I love."

Clint tipped his hat to the woman. She was pretty battered-looking right now but give her a week of rest and a doctor's care and she'd be pretty again. "See you in Denver, Claire."

As he rode away, he heard her call, "I'll pray you'll find them, Gunsmith! Maybe that'll work against you, me being what I was, but I'll pray it anyway!"

Clint touched spurs and returned his complete attention to the Arkansas River. He could see the trail of the crossbred herd when it angled down into the river and where they came out again on the north side. The cattle rustlers would be on their way to Denver. Hell, they'd probably be in Denver by now and the herd would be sold or already slaughtered.

A crying shame. But while he had grown to like those cattle, Mandy and Bart were the ones who really counted. And if they were alive, he meant to find them.

TWENTY-FIVE

He found the place where she had hidden under the bank, and two hours later he discovered where Mandy had climbed out of the Arkansas River and started north to follow her stolden herd of roan cattle.

When Clint overtook her, it was almost sunset and she had been sleeping in an old buffalo wallow. She had been hiding during the day and walking all night. And had he not chanced upon her getting to her feet in preparation for another night of travel, he could have ridden within fifty yards of her and never known of her presence.

"Mandy!"

She froze like a statue then seemed to recognize his voice. She was covered with dried mud and dead grass. Gaunt and weak, she looked like an escapee from hell. "Clint?"

He drove Duke forward and then hauled him into a sliding stop. Before the black gelding even came to a standstill, Clint was on his feet and running to the girl. He scooped her up in his arms and crushed her to his body. In between her sobs, she told him about the night raid, the death of her father, and how he had saved her life by standing up to the guns and then throwing her into the river.

"He wanted me to live, Clint. He loved me after all."

"I knew that. I'm glad you finally discovered the truth, Mandy."

"I want my cattle back. I want to find the men who murdered my father and see them hang."

"Did you see their faces?"

"No."

"It doesn't matter. If we can prove someone stole your cattle, a jury would also convict them of murder."

"But what if the cattle are already sold and on their way to market?"

"Then we try and find them before they are slaughtered. Mandy, they were too outstanding to have all gone to slaughter. Someone who knew cattle breeding would have seen and bought at least a few."

"That's what I've been hoping. But I just don't know."

Clint lifted her up into his saddle and climbed on behind. "We'll get to Denver and find those cattle. That's a promise."

She nodded wearily and Clint set Duke into a ground-eating jog. He didn't have enough money to buy a replacement horse for the poor Texas cowgirl. They would have to ride double all the way to Denver. But they'd do it easy enough because Duke was well rested and strong. Denver was only about a hundred miles northwest. Less than a two-day ride.

"God help them when I find them," Mandy whispered. "Do you have an extra gun?"

"Yeah. But this time, why don't you leave the gunplay to me? It's more in my line of work."

"I thought you were retired to gunsmithing."

"I am," he said. "But sometimes, I feel a strong need to test the tools of my trade."

"Is that what you did to get out of jail in Pueblo?"

He nodded. "With a little help from a young woman named Claire."

"Claire who?"

"I don't know. I never learned her last name."

"Where is she now?"

"On her way to Denver, same as we are."

"Is she pretty?"

Clint laughed out loud. "The last time I saw her, one of her eyes was swollen shut and both were purple. One side

TRAIL DRIVE TO MONTANA 135

of her face was all swollen up from a blow and she looked about as pretty as you look right now."

"I look terrible, don't I." It was not a question.

"You look alive and once you get a bath and some hot food, you'll look remarkably well."

They rode awhile in silence. "This Claire," Mandy finally said, "Is she in love with you?"

"No."

"Then why did she . . .."

Clint reached around and placed his fingers gently over her lips. "You ask too many questions and you talk too damned much. Let's just enjoy the night and think about getting your herd back when we reach Denver."

Mandy nodded and they rode north. Soon, Mandy slept and Clint had no difficulty at all holding her upright in the saddle and against his broad chest.

Dawn found them many miles north and Mandy did not awaken until midmorning.

"My God!" she said, blinking at the bright sun. "I slept all night!"

"And half the morning. You were tired. See that ranch up ahead?"

"Yes."

"I got a hunch," Clint said, "that there is a real nice family living there. The woman of the house is going to draw you a hot bath and you are going to scrub up while she washes your clothes and hangs them on the line to dry. Then, they are going to feed us a fine dinner before we leave."

"What makes you think that?"

"Because I have been to that little ranch before and I know the people. They are poor and could use some of the cash I have in my pocket."

"I see. Do you think we should stop and take that much time? I mean, my roan cattle could be . . ."

"Don't say it." Clint took a deep breath. "If they are gone, they are gone. But we need a rest and this horse could use the same. A good graining and brushing wouldn't hurt Duke either."

"Of course." Mandy reached out and patted Duke on the neck. "It was selfish of me to think only of myself. This horse is magnificent. He seems tireless and like he could keep jogging forever."

"Not quite, but almost," the Gunsmith said.

The ranch hospitality was every bit as good as Clint had remembered. This was a small family, one that raised a few head of beef and a truck-garden which they hauled to Denver and sold for ready cash. They were good people and when Clint and Mandy stood ready to leave, the man said, "I sure wish you'd take the loan of that old mare of ours, Gunsmith."

His name was Arthur Millbury and he was short with big, work-thickened hands and a perpetual squint from looking into the Colorado sun too many hours each day.

"I appreciate your offer," Clint replied, "but I can't do that. You need the mare yourself."

Mandy sat easy in the saddle. She was clean and her hair had been brushed. Her clothes were spotless and pressed. She looked like a new woman and color was back in her cheeks.

"I'll never forget you," she said to the woman who stood beside her two barefoot boys. "Your kindness or your carrot cake."

The woman handed up a sack of food. "You eat most of that and don't let the Gunsmith talk you out of the cake, my dear. You're a sight too skinny."

Clint grinned and waved good-bye. He had given the family seven dollars. Five dollars to Mr. Millbury and a dollar each to the two boys after making them promise not to tell where it came from. But hellfire, they'd earned it. They'd curried Duke and hand-fed him grain and hay like he was a toothless old dog. Now, the gelding stepped out with a new lift to his hooves that would carry them quickly across the next fifty miles.

TRAIL DRIVE TO MONTANA

Clint looked straight ahead toward Denver. He knew that most of the cattle rustlers would be the same crew that had taken him back into Pueblo with the sheriff.

I'll remember their faces, Clint thought. And when I see them, they'll also remember mine. It ought to be interesting.

TWENTY-SIX

Denver looked to Clint to be the biggest and most promising city in Colorado. It was the head of the county and the seat of all territorial business.

"I'd heard it was big," Mandy said as they rode Duke double down Larimer Street, "but I never thought it was like this!"

"They had a huge gold strike here in 1858 and when it finally died out, a lot of folks around here discovered they sort of liked this mountain city just for what it was all by itself. It boomed and then the Union Pacific Railroad decided not to build the transcontinental through here. That caused a lot of folks to fold up their tents and leave, but enough stayed and the city kept building. Now, the railroad has built a spur line all the way down from Cheyenne."

"So if they shipped my cattle, they'd go through Cheyenne on their way to the East."

"Or perhaps even West," Clint said. "There are some mighty big cattle raisers in Utah, Nevada, California, and Oregon that would like to introduce your crossbred blood into their own herds."

"Then the first place we ought to head is the stockyards," Mandy said.

Clint nodded. "That'd be the way I'd play this."

"Then let's find it," Mandy said eagerly.

Clint nodded. He rode through town until he came to the railroad tracks and then he followed them north to the huge

Union Stockyards. They stopped by the pens and surveyed what looked to be almost an ocean of cattle bound for distant markets. There was a long cattle train on the track and it was loading cattle as fast as they could be driven up into the flimsy-looking cattle cars that were little better than cheap corrals on wheels with a top on them.

Dust rose in a cloud over the entire mass of confusion and the noise of bawling cattle and cussing cowboys could be heard for miles. The stench traveled even farther.

"There must be twenty thousand here at least!"

But Clint shook his head. "No more than ten or twelve thousand. And there's nothing to do but start riding the alleys and searching the pens. It's a good thing that your herd will stand out so clearly."

As they rode through the maze of alleys, they studied each group of cattle, thinking that perhaps the herd had been split up to better hide its true origin and identity. They saw roan cattle, hundreds of them, but they were all the tall, bony longhorn variety, with their great, curved horns.

It took them almost two hours to search the stockyards and when they were satisfied that they could not have missed the crossbreds, Clint stopped an employee and said, "Miss Roe and I are searching for a herd of cattle."

"Red roan cattle," Mandy said, giving the dusty young cowboy her best smile. "They are stockier than the longhorns and uniform in size."

"You mean, they wasn't longhorns?"

"No," Mandy said, "they have some longhorn blood in them but other European beef breeds as well. They were different."

"Horned?"

"Yes. Have you seen anything like them?"

"I have."

"What happened to them?" Mandy said.

The cowboy stood up in his stirrups and took off his hat. He was young and very serious. "I think they may already have been shipped. But this section here is where I work and I keep no track of that part of the operation."

Mandy sagged with defeat. "Is there any way of telling for sure?"

"Not unless you got the name of the owner and a bill of sale."

"I had papers!" Mandy wailed. "They were stolen from me by cattle rustlers on the Arkansas River."

"Woo-wee," the cowboy said with a sad shake of his head. "Then you got no proof of ownership."

"I'm a witness to that the cattle belong to Miss Roe," Clint said. He patted the gun at his side. "And I got five little jurors in my Colt .45 that says I'll win when it comes time to hold court."

The cowboy nodded. "Can't blame you a bit," he said. "If they was my herd, I'd danged sure figure to do the same. But I was you, I'd go to the big boss of this whole sheee-bang and ask him about them cattle. You got to find 'em before anything else."

"Good point," Clint said. "So point your big boss out to us and we'll trouble you no more."

The cowboy smiled. He was boyishly good-looking and he could not seem to take his eyes off Mandy. "No trouble a-tall," he said with a bold wink. "Good luck, miss. You need more help, you call out for Billy Joe Meeker. Here me, now?"

"I hear you, Billy Joe. Thanks."

They rode on in the direction that had been pointed out to them. Clint said, "If you were wondering how you look anymore, I guess Billy Joe sort of answered that question."

"Aw," Mandy said with a shrug of her shoulders, "he was just a moon-faced kid with nothing better on his mind than having some fun under the stars."

The big boss was named Ed Seaver and they had no trouble finding him at all. Clint let Mandy describe the situation and when she was finished, he could see that Mr. Seaver was pretty upset.

"We bought those cattle intending to send them to

Chicago for slaughter but then people started noticing how big and uniform they were. Pretty quick, I had buyers coming out of the trees wanting that herd. I sold them to a man who has a ranch in Wyoming."

"Has he paid for them yet? Mister, they are stolen cattle."

"No, the man has not paid for them yet though they are being shipped. Can you prove any of what you are saying?"

Mandy bit her lower lip. "I think I can," she said. "My father was killed when the rustlers struck but there is a Dr. Thomas Thom down in Texas who has a copy of the pedigree and a description of each animal. A detailed description not only of physical size and markings, but of their bloodlines."

Seaver frowned. "Shoot," he swore. "We operate a clean yard here. I took pedigree papers on those cattle and I got a bill of sale."

"I can describe those papers, Mr. Seaver. I know them almost by heart. Cow number 101 is three years old with a small white spot near her udder and she has a funny way of swinging her back hoof when she walks. Cow number 102 has a busted horn but she might be one of the best of the lot. Her daddy was . . ."

"Whoa up there!" Seaver cried. "All right, I believe you! Just pay me back what I paid for that herd plus feed costs and we are square. I'll pass on the profit and inform my Wyoming buyer the cattle were rustled."

Mandy swallowed noisily. "Mister, I don't have any money left."

Seaver sighed. "Then I can't help you."

"Wait a minute," Clint said. "How much did you pay for the herd?"

"Twenty-five hundred dollars in cash," the stockyard boss said. "Feed bill will be another two hundred dollars. It'll cost you $2,700 altogether to get your herd back and you can sell them for a thousand dollars profit. That's how much I stand to make this afternoon for the stockyards."

Clint had exactly forty-three dollars and change in his worn Levi's and he knew Mandy did not have enough money

TRAIL DRIVE TO MONTANA 143

to run the total up to fifty dollars.

"The men that you paid. Are they still in town?"

"Hell if I know," Seaver said. "But when I dealt with them, one said something about the Cattleman's Hotel. Now, I got to get back to work. Young woman, I'll need that money by five o'clock or I'll have to turn the herd over to the buyer when he shows up with his money later this afternoon. Those cattle have to be shipped. I can't take the chance of getting stuck for another week's feed costs."

"We'll bring the money," Clint said.

Seaver shook his head. "I stand to lose a thousand dollars of profit, but if what you said is true, I'll do it gladly. Try the Cattleman's Hotel."

"We will," Clint said.

"Where are my cattle right now?"

"They are already on the train and ready to roll. You get the money here by five o'clock, we have time to get them unloaded before the train rolls out. After that . . . I'm sorry but I can't help you."

Mandy had a stricken look on her face. "Clint, I want to see them!"

He reined Duke around and headed back for town at a hard gallop. "No time, Mandy! We've only got a couple of hours to get that money!"

Mandy wailed but she did not protest. She knew the Gunsmith was right. Every minute counted. And if they could not find the cattle rustlers fast, they would have to come up with another way to get the cash. It was just that simple.

The Cattleman's Hotel was big and rambling. It had two stories. The second floor had its own sweeping balcony overlooking the South Platte River and the towering Rockies just west of town. Clint tied Duke to a long hitching rail in front of the hotel and adjusted the gun so that it rested nicely on his hip.

"I'll like to take that other Colt you're carrying," Mandy said.

"I'd as soon you left it to me and stayed out here."

"Not a chance," Mandy said. "We are talking about my cattle and my murdered father. I'm coming in, too."

Clint just nodded. He'd known all along that he could not stop her but he had needed to try. "All right, then you hide the gun in your skirt and stay away from me. If there is trouble, I want it to come at them from two directions."

"I'll pretend I'm a guest and wait in the lobby."

"Sounds good. I'll go into the hotel's saloon and look for our friends. Let's try to get the drop on them and avoid a shoot-out."

"Of course. But let's just hope they are still here."

Clint went in first and damned if he did not see two of them walking into the hotel's saloon the moment he stepped through the front door.

The hotel was big and fancy by the standards of the West. It had a hand-carved registration desk and fancy chandeliers hanging from the ceiling. The rugs were oriental and there were lots of ornate, gold-plated pictures of famous cattlemen and cattle on the walls. Clint was too preoccupied to notice Charles Goodnight and several other famous ranchers. He avoided the questioning glance of the desk clerk and headed for the saloon.

That's where the snakes were denned and waiting.

And it didn't matter whether or not their lair was humble or as fancy as there were in this place. These men were ruthless killers.

Clint patted the butt of his gun, pulled his dust-coated Stetson low on his forehead, and stepped into the saloon knowing that all hell was about ready to break loose.

TWENTY-SEVEN

There were five of them at the bar and Clint recognized them all. And since he had five bullets in his six-gun with the hammer resting on an empty, the Gunsmith figured he had a decent chance at whittling the odds no matter what these cattle-rustling murderers decided.

Clint glanced back into the lobby and nodded to Mandy who looked nervous but determined. When she started toward him, he turned and walked into the saloon with his gun loose and his stomach tight as a drum.

Clint pushed back his Stetson and said, "You five men are under arrest for the murder of Bart Roe and the stealing . . ."

That was as far as he got. They all wheeled around like the spokes on a wheel and two of them went for their guns. Clint drew and fired and both men died before their weapons cleared leather. "Freeze or you'll join them!"

The other three froze. They watched their dead companions topple to the floor and lie still. The entire roomful of men froze. A bald-headed bartender held a wet glass in his hand and it dripped soapy water into a sink behind the bar. Clint could hear each drop fall.

Someone moved into the saloon and, for an instant, Clint had a wild urge to turn but he held steady and said, "Mandy, keep your gun on them while I relieve them of their hardware."

"I will," she said in a voice that was higher pitched than

usual but held a note of angry determination.

Clint walked up to the three Pueblo outlaws and said, "Turn around and put your hands on the top of the bar. If you move them before I say so, I'll put a bullet hole through them."

The three men whirled and did as they were told.

Clint pulled their sidearms and then proceeded to shake them down. Besides their Colts, the men were carrying two knifes and one had a derringer in his vest pocket. "All right, now turn around slow and tell me a story."

They turned. The one in the center was taller than Clint and beefy. "We ain't saying a damn thing without talking to a lawyer."

"Is that right?" Clint smiled and stepped back a pace. "I'm going to start by blowing off your big toes," he said almost conversationally. "Did you know that, without the big toe, a man sort of walks off balance all the time? That's a fact. Now, just you hold still."

He pointed his six-gun at the man and pulled the trigger. The toe of the man's boot took the slug and the cattle rustler dropped and rolled on the floor while howling in pain. "Jesus Lord," he screamed, "you really did it!"

Clint did not think so. He had purposefully aimed just a hair out so that maybe his bullet had gone through the tip of the man's toenail, but that would be about all. Still, it was possible the man's boots were too small and he had shot off the whole toe.

"You," he said, pointing to the next man, "stick your foot out and hold it steady. I don't want to miss and put the next bullet through your foot."

The man threw himself up on his toes and cried, "Now wait a minute. Please! I'll talk. I am talking. Just tell me what you want to know!"

"I think you can guess. Tell the bartender and his patrons about the night raid you and these men made on this young woman and her father. Tell us how you rustled her herd and killed her father, Bart Roe!"

"I didn't do that! I swear it. Jesse and Mike was the ones that killed that old man. Not me! I was going after the cattle. We all was!"

Clint looked around at the other people who were staring. "You are all witnesses to this. Someone go find the sheriff. Tell him—and him alone—the Gunsmith has a couple of cattle rustlers for his jail."

Two men sprinted out of the saloon. Clint heard them yell across the hotel lobby, "Two men are dead and the Gunsmith has got the drop on some cattle rustlers!"

Clint groaned. He knew he had made a mistake. "Where are the rest of your friends?" he asked.

Mandy stepped forward. "First things first, Clint. Ask them for the money that Mr. Seaver paid them for my cattle."

"We ain't seen a penny of it," one of the outlaws hissed. "Jesse and Mike made sure we put every penny of it in the Denver bank."

Clint frowned. "You expect me to believe that?"

"Sure. You can't trust anybody anymore. We all watched him make the deposit. Four of us signed the deposit slip so that the money can't be taken out without all of us signing. We was supposed to do that tomorrow and split it even."

This was not what Clint wanted to hear. "All right, you and who else besides this Jesse and Mike have to sign."

The outlaw grinned wickedly. "Slim was the fourth and you just kilt him. That's him layin' there dead as a dog."

"Dammit!" Mandy exclaimed. "What are we going to do now?"

Clint frowned and started thinking. "Where are Jesse and Mike now?"

"Whorehouse just about two blocks over."

"Shut up, Harvey," the man with the hole in his toe screeched. "They'll kill us for this!"

"I'll kill you if you don't help us get that money within the next hour!" Mandy vowed. "Let's go get them."

Clint shook his head. "You can't go to a whorehouse."

But Mandy shook her head. "When are you going to learn you can't tell me where to go when it comes to my herd of crossbred cattle!"

Clint shrugged. "I just did."

He looked to the other patrons and the bartender. "We are going to take a walk with Harvey to find his friends. Will you hold the two I left breathing?"

"Sure," the bartender said, dragging a shotgun out and laying it across the bar. "They confessed, didn't they."

"Thanks," Clint said as he grabbed Harvey by his collar and propelled him toward the lobby. "I just hope that this Mike and Jesse don't get the word we are coming to get them before we arrive. They do, I'll use you for a shield."

"After the way I been cooperatin'!"

It was clear that Harvey thought he deserved special consideration. And maybe he did. Cattle rustlers were hanged if caught in the act. When arrested after the act, they usually spent about ten years in prison.

"If you behave and play this straight," Clint said, "I'll talk to the sheriff and have him recommend to the judge that you get a reduced prison sentence."

"How about a full pardon?"

Clint shook his head and prodded the man out the door of the Cattleman's Hotel. "How about you do exactly as I tell you and then we get that money out of the bank before it closes."

They heard a train whistle and Mandy looked to Clint who looked at his pocket watch. "We still got half an hour to go before five. We'll make it."

"But even if we get the money Mr. Seaver paid for those cattle, we still have to come up with the feed bill!"

"I know," Clint replied. "But dammit, one thing at a time, honey. First the big money, then the feed bill later. It'll work itself out somehow."

"I sure hope you're right," Mandy said, not sounding at all confident. "But we are cutting this mighty close."

● ● ●

TRAIL DRIVE TO MONTANA

They found the whorehouse and it was nothing but a dilapidated old cottage. What set it apart, besides the business that went on inside, was a neat white picket fence covered with wild red roses in full bloom.

"They are mighty pretty," Clint said as he marched Harvey up to the walk and knocked on the front door. Clint kept his gun barrel pressed tightly against Harvey's spine.

The door opened and a large, very buxom madam appeared. She was wearing too much rouge and perfume but she had a lovely smile. "Well, what do we have here! Two men and a pretty young woman. What is this, trouble or some kind of request for an unusual party?"

"It's a surprise party," Clint said, pushing his way inside and showing the woman his gun. "And if you and your girls just tell me which rooms Jesse and Mike are in, it'll stay peaceable. Please believe me, ma'am, I mean no harm but that pair are wanted for cattle rustling and murder. Now, where are they?"

The madam looked Clint over very carefully, then turned her attention on Mandy. "Who is she?"

"It was my father they murdered," Mandy said tightly. "And I mean to see them hang."

The madam thought that over and must have believed Mandy because she looked into her parlor at three scantily clad girls who were watching with round eyes. "Girls," she said, "I think you had better go quietly to your rooms and lock your doors until I knock and say that it is safe to come out again."

They left in a hurry.

"This way," the madam said courteously. "One of those you seek is in this room. One in that."

Clint had a dilemma. If he burst into one room, the other man might be able to escape. And if . . .

"I'll take this one," Mandy whispered with her gun up and ready. "Let's go."

"All right. Now!"

The doors were unlocked and Clint burst inside to see a

man making love to a fat woman. "Freeze!" he ordered, cocking his gun.

The man froze in a most embarrassing position. "Get dressed," Clint said, grabbing the man's gunbelt off the bed poster. "We're going to the bank!"

Two shots spun Clint around and he dashed back into the hallway to hear and see the second man, completely naked, holding his buttocks and dancing around a bed in helpless agony.

"You shot him in the act?" Clint asked, taking in the scene and the prostitute who lay on the bed trembling with fear.

Mandy nodded. "He was going for his gun. What else could I do?"

Clint shook his head and dashed back into the first room just as the man was about to grab the windowsill. "Hold it, this isn't over yet."

The man whirled on him. "Sheriff, you could have waited another thirty goddamn seconds," he hissed, his eyes going back to the fat girl. "Thirty seconds is all I needed."

"That's a real shame, mister. One you'll have ten years or more to think about if you don't go to the gallows."

The man looked at him with dull incomprehension.

"For what?"

"The murder of Bart Roe and the theft of those roan crossbred cattle."

He paled. It was obvious he had mistaken Clint for being a local law officer. Now, he looked sick at heart and very frightened. "If . . . if I give you a list of every man in Pueblo that is in on this, will it help me?"

"I don't know," Clint said. "But it can't hurt. You can give it to the sheriff and we'll take it from there. I imagine a U.S. marshal will be paying all those folks a surprise visit. But right now, let's go to the bank. Hurry up!"

They rushed down the street, but the man with a hole in his buttocks was screaming bloody murder and he slowed their progress considerably. When they marched into the bank, Clint expected a commotion and was not disappointed. It took a full ten minutes to calm everyone down enough to explain that they wanted to make a $2,500 withdrawal. Clint had the foresight to learn Slim's real name and that the man had been illiterate. Slim had used a simple X for his signature. It made forging his mark real easy.

"What time is it?" Mandy cried as they rushed out the bank.

"A quarter to five," Clint replied.

"And we are still short the two hundred dollars for Mr. Seaver's feed bill!"

Clint turned his gun on the three men, and though he knew this was entirely illegal, he said, "Empty your pockets of all your money! Hurry Up!"

"You're robbing us?" Harvey asked in disbelief.

"That's about the size of it."

They had almost a hundred dollars between them and, with Clint's own money and what little Mandy kicked into the pot, it added up to nearly a hundred and fifty.

"Still fifty short," he said when he had finished counting.

The sheriff was coming. Clint saw him and knew there was no time to answer all the lawman's questions. Not if he was going to get those crossbred cattle off the train before they pulled out.

"Here," he shouted to Mandy as he shoved his gun at her. "Hold them for the sheriff and I'll meet you at the Union Stockyards!"

"But . . . where are you going?"

"I know of only one person in Denver who might help me!" he shouted as he raced down the street. He was going to find a girl named Claire who worked at the Red Onion Café.

TWENTY-EIGHT

Clint had thought he'd seen the Red Onion Café on Larimer Street when he had ridden into town but he could not be sure. He'd been so preoccupied with his thoughts about Mandy and her missing herd of crossbreds that he really had not been paying too much attention.

But now, as he dashed down the crowded street, glancing up and down the boardwalks at the dozens of flourishing businesses, he spotted the café. He had to run a hundred more yards and he was almost out of breath when he burst inside.

"Clint Adams!"

Claire almost dropped a platter of beef and steaming potatoes on a customer before she set it down and rushed to throw her arms around Clint's neck and give him a big kiss. "Boy, is it good to see you again!"

He broke free of her and grinned. All the customers grinned, too, as she practically dragged him into the kitchen.

"Margaret, this here is the man I was telling you about. The one who saved my . . . my neck from that deputy in Pueblo."

Margaret was at least ten years older, her face was lined, and her forehead was damp from cooking in the hot kitchen. But it was clear she had been a handsome woman in her youth and there was a strong resemblence between the pair.

Margaret wiped her hands on a greasy towel and shoved one out to Clint. "Claire told me what you did for her. I wished she'd have told me about that bastard named Latigo, I'd have come down to Pueblo and killed him."

Claire shrugged, "She's still the big sister, Clint. Always trying to look out for me."

Margaret returned to her griddle and sizzling steaks. "She needs someone to look after her! You hungry, Clint?"

"Yes, ma'am, I mean, but I sort of have an emergency right now. I need to borrow some money."

Margaret glanced at him. She looked disappointed. "Sure you do. All right, how much?"

"Fifty dollars," the Gunsmith said, feeling embarrassed to have to make the request. "And I'll give you something to hold until I can pay you back."

"No!" Claire said hotly. "I have some money and some wages coming. Give him what I'm due, Margaret, and I'll make up the rest."

"Then what are you going to live on?"

"Never mind," Clint said. "I'll find it somewhere else even if I have to sell my damn saddle."

But Claire grabbed him and led him to the cash register. She pulled money out of her own pockets and then carefully added enough to total fifty dollars. "You're in a big hurry," she said as she counted the money once more. "I can tell you are so I'll not ask why you need this so bad. All I ask is that you come when I lock the doors to this place at ten o'clock and tell me then."

"I will," he said. "I sure hope I didn't cause any trouble between you and your sister."

Claire kissed him again. "There has always been trouble between us. She treats me like I was twelve years old. Maybe I need that and maybe not. But you need this money so, git!"

"You sure healed up in a hurry. You look pretty again, Claire."

"I fell pretty now that I am making an honest day's wages. Now, go on. Skeedaddle!"

Clint did not need any urging. He bolted out the door

TRAIL DRIVE TO MONTANA 155

and headed on the run for the Cattleman's Hotel where Duke was waiting. When he reached his horse, he untied him and swung into the saddle and headed for the Union Stockyards at a hard gallop.

Billy Joe Meeker came riding hard down the alleys to meet him. "You lookin' for Mr. Seaver, the Big Boss?"

"Yes, where is he?"

"Waitin' for you, Gunsmith. We been waiting by that boxcar of roan cattle for almost an hour now, hoping you'd show. Heard all over town about your shoot-out at the Cattleman's Hotel. Why didn't you tell me you were so damned famous!"

Clint headed for the train at a gallop. "Because I don't feel famous," he said to the young cowboy who rode tall beside him.

He pulled Duke up beside the stockyard boss just as the train jolted into motion. "Hey, wait!" Clint shouted. "I have the money."

"I'm sorry," Seavers said. "I held the Union Pacific up just as long as I could but they have a schedule to keep."

"The hell with their schedule!" Clint raged. "We've gone through too damn much to quit now. If I stop the train, will you help me unload those cattle?"

"I can't," Seavers said. "I'd lose my job. I got a wife and kids. I just can't do it."

"I can," Billy Joe Meeker said. "You stop that train, make them back it to the chute, and I'll get into those boxcars and have those roan cattle out in thirty minutes."

Seavers shook his head. "I can't allow that, Billy Joe. You work for me and I have to order you to stay out of this."

"I won't. Gunsmith, stop the locomotive before it gathers up steam and runs away from us!"

Clint reined Duke and shot off after the train. There were twenty-five cattle cars and they were all bulging with beef. That meant it would take a long ways before the train could gather momentum.

Clint and Duke thundered past cattle car after cattle car

and when he passed the coal tender, he yelled at the fireman and the engineer, "Stop this train!"

The noise of the steam engine drowned out his words and, even had they been heard, it would be unlikely they'd have obeyed. They both looked at the Gunsmith and shrugged. The engineer yelled something at his fireman and the man began to shovel more coal into the firebox.

Clint knew that Duke could not keep up the pace much longer. They were two miles out now and the train was slowly picking up steam pressure and speed. He did the only thing he could do and that was to jump from his horse and grab ahold of the coal tender.

It wasn't hard and Duke swung sharply away from the tracks, happy to put a distance between himself and the smelly, hissing engine. Clint unholstered his gun and pointed it at the Union Pacific engineer. "I said to stop this damned train!"

Funny how a man heard so well when he had a gun pointed at his brains. The engineer leapt for the brake and drew the train to a shuddering standstill.

"Now," Clint said, his gun still on the railroading man. "There has been a terrible mistake and the fifth through the ninth cattle cars back are holding a rustled herd of roan cattle. They have to be returned to the stockyards and unloaded."

"But we got a schedule to keep!" the engineer shouted.

"I know. But like the old saying goes: better late than never. Savvy my meaning?"

The engineer savvied just fine. He put the train in reverse and they headed back to town every bit as fast as they had departed.

Clint watched Billy Joe work the cattle. The young man was a whirlwind of efficiency. He would signal when each car was exactly in position, then leap up into them and vanish into the car. A moment later, roan cattle would come flying out to race down the chute.

Clint shook his head in wonder. He could not understand

how come the crossbred bulls did not gore or stomp him to death. But then, that was the difference between a cowboy and a gunsmith.

Mandy came racing up, and after a few words, Clint saw the pair of them to go to work. All in all, it took them less than a half an hour to unload the Texas herd.

That done, they signaled to Clint and raised their fists in triumph. "You can head north for Cheyenne again," Clint said. "And thanks for being so understanding."

"Go to hell!" the engineer said.

"Nope, got to get to Montana first."

"Then go to hell!"

Clint smiled and swung down to the prairie. He stepped back and the steam whistle shrieked in anger and the big driving wheels churned. Slowly, the train pulled away and he watched it until it vanished in the northern horizon.

Duke came up to nuzzle his shoulder and the Gunsmith scratched his horse behind the ear. "Good race," he said, "And I'd like to tell you that this cattle driving business is all over, but it's not. We still got another four or five hundred miles to take those red critters. Think you can stand up to another few weeks of playing cowhorse?"

The black gelding nodded its head and started munching contentedly on brown bunch grass.

TWENTY-NINE

Mandy and Clint sat beside the campfire and watched the embers die. They could hear Billy Joe singing to the herd as he rode around and around the contented cattle.

"He sings real pretty, don't he, Clint?"

"He does for a fact." Clint finished his coffee and smiled. "That man is a real cowboy. I never seen anyone handle cattle like he does. I think someone that good with them has a gift."

"You'll learn," Mandy said with encouragement. "It just takes times."

"I don't want to spend the time," Clint said softly. "I want to travel and see things. I think we've gone over this a time or two."

She nodded. "We have. But forgive me for wanting to forget. I just keep hoping."

"Mandy, one of the saddest and most common mistakes a man or a woman can make is to marry someone thinking they will remake their new husband or wife. It happens, I guess, about one time out of a hundred—if that often. The rest of the time it causes a whole lot of anger and pretty soon it's just a matter of who gives up on who—the one who is trying to be the changer, or the one who don't want to get changed. You understand what I'm trying to tell you? Cowboyin' just isn't what I am cut out to do. I'd never be as good as Billy Joe even if I worked hard at it for a hundred years."

She barely managed a smile. "Maybe, maybe not. But I care for you, Clint."

"And I feel the same. But it's time to let go a little and look to a greener pasture. You might start by getting better acquainted with your new cowboy."

"You mean just ride out there and start talking with him?"

"Sure! Maybe you both could even start singing from opposite sides of the herd and sort of work your way around toward each other."

Mandy glanced out toward the herd. "I do know that song and he sure sings it pretty."

"So go on and tell him and then sing with him."

"What about you?"

"I'll be fine. Go on now."

Mandy got up. "I feel a little funny just riding out there in the dark with a stranger."

"I have a feeling he won't let you stay a stranger for long. He gave up a pretty good job to help us. That took something special."

"Yeah. I guess it did, didn't it!"

Clint watched her saddle her horse and ride out into the dark. He stretched, saddled Duke, and headed out in the opposite direction toward Denver. About a mile out, he heard the pair break into "Git Along Little Doggies."

They sang a real pretty duet.

"You came," she said as she locked the door of the Red Onion Café and hugged him tightly. "I was afraid you wouldn't."

"Why?"

"I just was. Would you like to see the little house my sister rents me out behind her own big house?"

"Nothing I could think of I'd rather do," Clint said as he offered her his arm and they strolled along the boardwalk.

A pair of drunk cowboys leered and one started to make some crude remark but Clint thumbed back his Stetson and heard the other whisper in a panic, "It's the Gunsmith,

Carl. For God's sake shut your trap!"

Both men tipped their hats as Clint and Claire passed on by.

Claire smiled with amusement. "Do men always treat you like that?"

"Sometimes. Almost always after I have just killed someone."

"I see."

They walked on in silence until they entered a nice residential area and then then came to a large brick house.

"My sister and her husband live here. I live in the back. Come on."

They tiptoed around the house and Claire unlocked her door as quiet as she could but, back at the front, Clint saw the bedroom curtains shift and caught a glimpse of Margaret.

"She saw us," he said as he entered a neat but very Spartan little room.

"Then she'll not sleep well until you leave."

"Maybe I better not stay long," Clint said.

But she took her head and melted into his arms.

"Margaret will live with a little less sleep. But I haven't had a man since the Pueblo. Been saving it for you, Gunsmith."

She lit a candle beside her bed. Next, she unbuttoned her blouse and then stripped right down to her creamy white skin. Clint smiled with admiration. He admired her large, firm breasts. Her girlishly slim hips and long legs were perfect. "You are pretty everywhere," he said.

"I'll bet you are, too."

Clint locked the door, for he did not trust Margaret. He glanced at the windows and made sure that the curtains were pulled tight. Then, he unbuckled his gunbelt and shucked out of his clothes feeling Claire's eyes hungry on him.

He heard her swallow dryly and she licked her lips. "When I did it for money, it was never any good. Now . . . with you for free, I feel like a virgin once more."

"You look like one, too," he said, moving close and

easing her down on the bed. "And that's the way I'll take you."

He kissed her breasts and she giggled and then cried out with delight. His fingers explored all the places and she squirmed and began to breathe hard as if it were the first time she had ever been intimately touched. And when he slipped his long middle finger into her womanhood, she was wet and warm.

"Ohhh," she breathed, pulling him down onto her.

"I'm going to go wild with you tonight. Put it in. Don't make me suffer like this. I might die of ecstasy!"

But Clint worked her with his finger another few minutes until she was begging for him. And when her moans became so loud that Margaret could not help but hear them, Clint raised himself up and took her like a virgin, slow and with great tenderness. But Claire grabbed his buttocks when she could not stand the exquisite pleasure he dealt her so carefully. She screamed with joy and began to pump her hips up and down and now Clint drove at her with a long, powerful stroke that sent her clawing at his back.

He felt her climax almost immediately and when she started to go limp, he said, "Don't rest, honey, this is only starting for you."

She laughed with happiness. "It was never like this. Not even the very first time!"

Clint nibbled at the lobes of her ears. His manhood kept stroking her and their bodies grew slick with perspiration.

"Oh, Clint, here it comes again!"

He felt her stomach muscles begin to twitch and he said, "This one will be even stronger, Claire."

"I'm afraid I can't stand it!"

But she did. And when they exploded together, it was like she had always dreamed it should be but never could be when it was for money instead of love. Clint filled her and fulfilled her through that long, passionate night of lovemaking.

The next morning when he strode out, he saw Margaret peering at him through the kitchen window.

She looked haggard and drawn but the Gunsmith felt completely revitalized—just like a sixteen-year-old kid again. He winked at the old jailkeeper and started whistling a cowboy tune.

THIRTY

It was a hundred and sixty miles from Denver to Cheyenne and they made it in ten days without pushing the crossbreds too hard. If they'd had the shipping fare, they'd have loaded the cattle back on the Union Pacific and freighted them to Cheyenne. Instead, they paralleled the railroad about five miles out and followed it north.

The season had changed from summer to fall by the time they reached Wyoming Territory. The nights were always cold now and the north wind had a bite. In the mornings, the brown grass was covered with frost and the cattle moved a little stiffly. To the northwest, the Laramie Mountains were already capped with the first winter's snow.

Mandy's cattle attracted a great deal of attention in Cheyenne. She sold fifteen head of cows and five bulls for an average of one hundred dollars each. And had she wanted to, Clint supposed that she could have sold at least that many more.

"I hated to sell a single one of them," she confessed ruefully. "But we needed food and supplies. Some winter coats, gloves, and boots. More blankets and woolen underwear. Besides, I didn't want to arrive at Uncle Milton's old homestead flat broke with winter chilling our bones."

"Good thinking," Clint said as he tried on a heavy wool coat and gloves. "A body can freeze to death in this country."

"And starve," Mandy said. "Also, I promised to pay Billy Joe a cowboy's wages."

The young man's cheeks colored. He and Mandy had struck up quite a romance and there was a full courtship in bloom that Clint found both touching and a little amusing.

"The wages ain't important," Billy Joe said. "You know I'm not here for the money."

Now it was Mandy's turn to blush. Clint looked away. He felt good knowing that this couple could do just fine once they reached Mandy's new Montana ranch. They would certainly not need him around all winter.

When they reached the south fork of the Powder River, Mandy felt as if they were almost home—but Clint knew better. It was still a good two hundred and fifty miles and he was concerned. The nights were getting so cold that the streams iced along their muddy banks.

"Quit worrying," Mandy said. "It is still only October."

Clint could only smile. Down in the southern part of Texas where Mandy was raised, October was the time of year when cottonwoods were finally starting to change color. But this far north, many of the trees stood bare and the leaves were falling heavily.

"I just don't want to get caught in a blizzard out here on this damned flat prairie."

"Maybe we should angle west toward those pretty mountains," Mandy suggested.

Clint shook his head. They were the Big Horns and following along their base would carry them much too far to the west.

Billy Joe Meeker agreed. "We need to get to your ranch as straightaway as we can, Mandy. You don't know these winters up here. Why, in Denver, the blizzards come awhippin' out of Kansas and they cut you to the quick. Might even be worse up here."

"It is worse," Clint said. "But this is sure pretty country."

"It's cattle country for certain," Mandy said. "And if I didn't already have a ranch waiting, then I'd think about staking out some of this grass."

That afternoon, Clint shot an antelope; they were as plentiful in Wyoming as jackrabbits were in Texas. The meat was delicious and it lasted them almost four days as they followed the Powder River northeast toward Montana and the Yellowstone River.

The first winter snowstorm to hit them struck them soon after they entered Montana Territory. It came like a ghost in the night and they did not expect it. Clint awoke cold and shivering and when he peeked out from under his covers, he saw the snow falling.

He pushed himself stiffly out of his bedroll and felt the hard wind coming down from the northeast. Clint was no expert on blizzards, but he figured this one had some teeth in it.

"Better get up and saddle your horses," he said, nudging Mandy and Billy Joe. "I think we have a problem coming at us head-on."

"We need to keep them moving," Billy Joe said a few minutes later. "Got to turn them with their backs to the wind."

"But that isn't the way we want to go!" Mandy shouted.

"Can't be helped. They won't drive into the storm, Mandy."

Clint did not argue. It made no sense for a man or a beast to face into a driving snowstorm. He heard thunder in the darkness and it was so cold he had a hard time cinching Duke for the ride. But he managed and climbed into his saddle. Head down, collar turned up to his ears, Clint pointed Duke toward the herd. The crossbreds were up and moving before the storm. Their backs were coated with fresh snow and their heads hung low.

A few hours later, the wind began to shriek. Clint did not know what time of night it was at the height of the storm. He just huddled in his saddle and gave Duke his head. The poor horse moved along with the herd, tail whipping between his legs.

Daylight was a sorry affair without warmth. The sun seemed to be buried in gray muslin as it peered timidly through heavy storm clouds. The temperature was well below freezing.

"Let's turn them back toward the Powder and head them north!" Billy Joe yelled, his breath creating big clouds of steam.

The snow had stopped falling but now the wind was coming straight out of the north and driving right into their faces. Clint looked over at Mandy and she looked like a snow sculpture. But she pulled down a woolen scarf and smiled.

"Aren't you glad we bought winter gear in Cheyenne?"

Clint nodded. "Are you thinking we should have stayed in Texas?"

Mandy shook her head. "I ain't afraid of this Montana country, and neither are my cattle."

"She's pretty but she's hard," Clint said to Billy Joe.

The cowboy winked and replied in a voice low enough that Mandy could not hear, "Never was a horse that couldn't be rode, never was a cowgirl who couldn't be throwed."

"That might be true, but right now all I care about is to arrive at that ranch and put my feet up before a roaring fireplace."

"You staying the winter?"

"Nope." Clint brushed snow off of his hat and replaced it firmly on his head. "Just long enough to thaw out and then get out."

Billy Joe laughed. "I'd do exactly the same if she wasn't so damned pretty and sweet!"

Clint looked to the north. He wondered how much longer it would be before they arrived at this ranch. He figured that would depend a great deal on the weather. If they kept being hit by blizzards, they would be in real trouble. But if they could get just one week of clear weather, then they would be on homeground. He was not a praying man but Clint said a little prayer for clear sailing this last couple of hundred miles. And just as soon as they arrived, he was going to thaw out one day and rein Duke south the very next.

To warmer country. Maybe even to visit his favorite Mexican senorita and bask in winter sunshine.

THIRTY-ONE

Bowtree, Montana, sat just below the confluence of the Powder and Big Horn Rivers. This was huge land, majestic and hard. Lumpy gray clouds stretched in any direction as far as the eye could see and it seemed to Clint that a man could go forever without bumping into another human being. But, of course, that was not true. Clint had learned that no matter how big the land, if it was rich with grass, there would be cattlemen laying a claim to it.

"I'll stay with the herd," Billy Joe Meeker said. "You two enjoy yourselves in town."

Mandy nodded as she and the Gunsmith rode away. "He won't hardly leave them cattle of mine for even a minute. I never saw a man like that before. He's some kind of cowboy, isn't he, Clint?"

"Yes, he is." Clint studied the town just ahead.

It was very small, probably had a population of about six hundred if you included the yard-dogs and horses. "Do you think your ranch should be close by?"

"I sure hope so. All I want to do is to get a land description and the boundaries and then feast my tired Texas eyes on it."

"Amen," Clint said. "So let's get a move on." He touched spurs to Duke and they galloped the rest of the way into town.

The first thing that the Gunsmith noticed was that there was no sheriff's office. That was not too surprising because towns this size generally had to rely on a U.S. marshal and a traveling circuit judge when there was trouble. And since that was always considered far too much bother, these small frontier communities generally meted out justice as they saw fit. Killers and horse thieves were hung on the spot, lesser crimes might warrant anything from being tarred and feathered to being whipped, dragged at the end of a rope, or even plain old stomped half to death. Frontier justice was swift, sometimes cruel, but damn near always highly effective.

"Why is it," Mandy asked, "that there is never a church or a schoolhouse in towns like this but always three or four saloons?"

"Because there aren't enough strong women to put up a fuss yet. But I'll bet you do, Mandy."

She smiled wearily. "I'll make some changes after I take care of my own problems this first winter. You know, Clint, once our crossbreds demonstrate how well they can get through these northern winters, we'll be on our way. Every rancher in Montana will be after me for a bull or a few heifers to breed into their herd."

"That's what I like about you," Clint said, "your confidence."

"Without it, I'd be nothing. That's what made my father as great as he was. He never asked what the odds against doing a thing were, he just tackled everything in life as if he knew he was going to beat it. I try to follow that very same kind of thinking."

It was not a bad way of going through life, Clint thought. Anyway, it sure beat fretting about every problem and trying to convince yourself that you couldn't overcome it.

They came to a small business with a lawyer's shingle hanging outside. It read: "Ronald Milligan, Esq. Attorney at Law." Below that, another sign proclaimed: "Expert in land contracts and litigation. I work good and cheap."

"Sounds like our man," Clint said as he reined Duke to a halt and dismounted.

"He better work real cheap." Mandy dismounted and

tied her horse up with a frown. "My pa, he always said to stay away from these fork-tongued son of a bitches. But then, maybe if he'd have had a few contracts in writing, he'd still have at least part of his ranch."

"Good morning!" Ronald Milligan said expansively as he offered them his thin, blue-veined hand. He was fiftyish, with gray hair and a long, gaunt body. As homely as a horse, he reminded Clint a little of Abraham Lincoln. "What can I do for you?"

Mandy did not mince her words. She quickly explained who she was and the reason she had come all the way to Montana. "I can't use you today, Mr. Milligan, but I promise you a fee when my first legal problem arrives."

He scratched his nose with the fingernail of his forefinger. "Miss Roe, I am afraid that you already have a 'legal problem'. You see, Mr. Benjamin Fistak already has claim to the land that your uncle once owned."

"What!"

Clint grabbed Mandy's arm. "Let's just hear him out."

"I'm sorry. He claims that the ranch was abandoned and, therefore, it is his right to file claim on it."

"I never heard of such a thing," Clint said.

"It's a county law on our books," the lawyer explained. "You see, at one time, there was a homestead law so generous that we had a slew of sod busters come into this country. They believed they could be successful here, but of course they all failed. The soil is too thin, the summer growing season much too short. In order to get the land reverted back to the county, we passed this ten-year abandonment and reversion law. Now, after ten years, the land reverts back to the territory and can be filed upon by anyone able to pay the back taxes."

"It hasn't even been ten years since it was abandoned!"

"I'm afraid it has."

"Dr. Thom said *nearly* ten years. He is very precise when he speaks. If it was ten years or over ten years, he would have said that very precisely."

"Yes," Clint said gently. "But we said good-bye to the good doctor almost three months ago."

Mandy blinked. Her face reflected all her sudden, crushing doubts. "Mr. Milligan, where is your cemetery?"

Milligan's eyes widened. "Of course! If his gravemarker wasn't carved of wood, it would still be in existence! With the dates of birth and death."

Milligan snatched up his coat and hat. "Come with me and I'll help you find it."

The cemetery was small and not well kept. The people of the West did not seem to have time to attend to the dead, they could hardly cope with making things bearable for the living. They found the grave of Milton D. White and the dates of his birth and death.

"My heavens!" the lawyer said with a loud gasp. "Your uncle died exactly ten years ago tomorrow!"

Clint shook his head in amazement while Mandy shuddered as if touched by her dear uncle's spirit. She said, "I almost feel . . . standing here, as if he has been pulling me and my herd every mile we have traveled from Texas. That's why we have pushed so hard. Never stopped to rest. He knew I had to be here by tomorrow!"

Milligan nodded. "Come on back to my office and I'll make out the filing papers. Yours will take precedence over those of Mr. Fistak after they are signed and notarized. But you must be on the premises and remain there a reasonable period of time in order to establish your right of survivorship."

"Oh," Mandy vowed. "We'll stay."

"Young woman, perhaps I should tell you that Benjamin Fistak is a very, very hard man. He believes he has made a legal and binding claim to that six thousand acres that your uncle homesteaded. He will not take this news in good spirits."

"I don't care how he takes it," Clint said. "We come

too damn far to give it up now. The land belongs to Mandy and she will decide to keep or sell it as she chooses."

"But, Mr. Adams, I have to tell you with great sadness that this country has only one law and that is of the gun. I abhor violence and do all I can to convince people that they need to work within a legal framework that is completely impartial and fair to all. But men like Mr. Fistak do not listen and I cannot have it on my conscience if you are . . . shot or in some other way dissuaded to remain in Montana."

Clint smiled. "You use mighty big words but they all boil down to one thing—Mr. Fistak is top dog in these parts and growls loudest."

"He also bites," Milligan said. "He has very large and sharp fangs."

Clint just shrugged. "I don't guess we're exactly toothless ourselves, are we?"

"Hell no, we aren't. Let him come tomorrow and try to get us off. We'll be ready!"

Ronald Milligan nodded. "Fine. I'll quickly draw up the papers and, with your advance of my fee, use that money to hire a livery and set out for the county seat to file your papers."

"Then you won't be here tomorrow?"

Milligan shook his head. "Heavens no! Once Mr. Fistak discovers what I've done, he'd string me up from the tallest tree by the . . . the toes and let the buzzards have me!"

Clint and Mandy exchanged concerned glances. It seemed that their trials were not quite over yet.

THIRTY-TWO

"My God!" Mandy whispered, her face going pale. "That can't be dear old Uncle Milton's ranch house!"

Billy Joe raised his eyebrows and looked at Clint, who managed to say, "Just needs a little work is all, honey. The rock fireplace still looks solid."

"But, Clint! It could snow any day!"

Billy Joe spurred his pony toward the tumble-down ranch house. The porch had fallen in and so had part of the roof. But at least one end of the house was still standing—the end the huge rock fireplace seemed to support.

"Shoot," the young cowboy said, "my pa spent most of his life rebuilding houses and stores that never looked this good even when they were brand spanking new."

"Your father was a carpenter?" Clint was surprised. It just didn't seem that a natural cowboy like Billy Joe could really be the son of a wood worker.

"Anything wrong with that?" Billy Joe asked, with a slight edge to his voice.

"Hell no!" Clint said with a grin. "I was just wondering how we were going to fix this place up, you a cowboy, Mandy a cowgirl, and me a gunsmith."

"Well," Billy said, "though I don't advertise the fact, I learned everything my father knew and I can handle a hammer and a saw almost as well as a rope. We'll get some tools and a few nails and have this place fixed up in a hurry."

"The corrals are still up," Clint said.

Mandy rode over to the well and cranked an oaken bucket up on a new rope. "Looks like someone—probably Mr. Fistak—has kept the well clear and clean. Water is sweet as corn syrup."

She placed her hands on her hips and surveyed the hay barn. "Cattle are going to have to forage for themselves this year. But they'll have things better next. This is damned good land, Clint. I mean to hang on to it."

"I'm glad to hear that," he said. "I think you can do very well here with your herd."

"I know she can," Billy Joe said.

"Then let's get started." Clint dismounted and watered Duke. He put the gelding into the pole corral and they let the small herd of crossbreds graze on the thick, dry grass. Billy said it didn't look like much, but it was plenty good for cattle feed. Clint did not doubt for a single minute that the Colorado cowboy knew just what he was talking about.

They set about cleaning out the place and ripping away the boards that would have to be replaced. Mandy rode back into town and returned two hours later with the owner of the town's general store and a wagonload of supplies and tools.

"You folks ought to wait until you have seen Mr. Fistak and his boys," the man warned. "He might change your mind about staying here."

"No he won't," Mandy said, grabbing a broom and heading for the house. "Thanks for dropping everything to come right back out with me."

The man nodded. "Thanks for the business. And, good luck—you'll need it when Fistak and his son, Ralph, learns what you are doing! That Ralph is a young brawler if there ever was one."

Clint frowned at the man who drove his wagon back toward Bowtree. "This Benjamin Fistak sure has everyone buffaloed in this country."

"Yeah," Billy Joe said. "And Ralph doesn't sound to be much friendlier."

"We'll just face them when the time comes," Clint said. "Until then, we got our work cut out for us."

They worked past dark until they could not see and then they quit and laid their bedrolls down before the fireplace. Using discarded timber, they built a nice bonfire and it was the first time that Clint was warm in days. He was reminded that he'd promised himself one day to thaw out and then he'd ride south. That did not look to happen.

In the morning, they arose to find light snow on the ground but the crossbred cattle were pawing it away and eating well. They had a quick breakfast and went back to work, their minds and thoughts completely occupied by the task of building a couple of winter-tight rooms that they could get by with until next spring when Mandy and Billy Joe planned to rebuild the fallen-in part of the house from the ground up.

It was about noon when Clint saw the riders come galloping through their roan herd of cattle, scattering them like quail.

"They shouldn't have done that," Billy Joe said, laying down his hammer and reaching for his gunbelt. "You scatter cattle a few times, they'll start running whenever they see approaching horsemen. If they are cattlemen, they ought to know better."

Clint placed a new saw down on the floor and buckled his own gunbelt down tight. "I don't think they give a damn what our cattle do," he said. "Unless I miss my bet, this is Ben Fistak and his son Ralph, along with their hands."

"I won't be threatened," Mandy said. She grabbed her own Colt and shoved it into her pocket. "Not a bit, I won't!"

Benjamin Fistak was approaching sixty years old but he still had a working man's body. He was short and powerful with a great bull neck and a red face. He wore a walrus mustache and a little pair of wire glasses that looked ridiculous perched on his huge, hooked nose.

The old man hauled his big palomino horse up in the yard and spat a long stream of tobacco. "What the hell do you think you are doing!" he bellowed. "Get off my land!"

"It is my land, Mr. Fistak. I am Milton D. White's niece and I have filed my claim of ownership to this land. I have the legal right of survivorship, Mr. Fistak, and you and your men are trespassing."

"Me!" The old man began jabbing his thumb against his chest over and over. "Me, trespassing! Get off this land!"

"No," Mandy said.

There were six of them and they looked determined. Especially the young man with the stamp of a Fistak written all over his square, heavy features.

"Ralph! You move them!"

Ralph Fistak simply nodded and went for his gun. And for a man as squatty and stupid as he appeared, he was deceptively fast. So fast and so unexpected that Clint barely recovered in time to draw his own gun and yell, "Hold it!"

Ralph again surprised him by freezing in the middle of his draw. He stared at Clint and swallowed nervously. He spoke for the first time. "The man is a gunfighter, Pa. He'll kill me if I go after him. What shall I do now?"

Benjamin snorted with rage and looked to his other three men. They knew what he wanted, but when Mandy and Billy Joe pulled iron, the three raised their hands and one said, "We didn't hire on to die for you, Mr. Fistak. We're cowboys and this ain't part of the deal."

"Cowards!" Fistak bellowed. He jumped off his palomino and charged Clint. The Gunsmith ducked a whistling overhand that would have dropped a horse had it connected.

Clint slipped a second punch. "Why don't you get ahold of your temper, Mr. Fistak. Mandy has legal claim to this ranch. Her uncle left it to her and we've driven that little herd of cattle all the way from Texas to start over here."

"Fight me with your fists, gunman!" Fistak whirled and came back swinging. Clint knew that the powerful old rancher outweighed him by fifty pounds and his punch would be lethal. So the Gunsmith did the smart thing, he pistol-

TRAIL DRIVE TO MONTANA 181

whipped Fistak hard enough to drop him to his knees.

During the many years of Clint's law career, he had always been amazed how a gunbarrel properly laid against a foolish man's skull slowed him down and got him to rethink his murderous intentions.

It worked now with Fistak. The rancher groaned and tried to rise but he was wobbly and there was no fight left in his eyes.

"Here," Clint said, reaching out to help the man up. "Let me . . ."

He didn't finish. Ralph jumped forward and bashed Clint across the back of the head and sent him facedown into the dust. Clint saw stars and then he heard Billy Joe shout just before the loud smack of fist on flesh.

Clint rolled over in the dirt and watched Ralph go after Billy Joe Meeker. Billy was ready, willing, and eager. He came back at Ralph with fists flying and the two stood toe to toe and battled like gladiators.

Ralph was far heavier but Billy was taller and had the reach and hand speed. They just kept trading punches until blood started to flow down their faces. First Ralph would knock Billy a few paces back, then Billy would find some new fire in his blood and come swirling back to deliver two and even three snapping punches to the heavier man's face.

"Stop it!" Mandy shouted, firing her gun again and again. "Stop it before you two idiots beat each other to death!"

They stopped swinging and stepped back to eye each other balefully. Their noses were both dripping blood and their lips were pulpy and torn.

They were both swaying but neither had the look of men willing to quit first.

Mandy shoved her gun into her holster and strode to the well. She yelled, "Give me a hand, boys!"

All three of Fistak's cowboys jumped to help and they carried the sloshing oaken pail back and held it while Mandy used a couple of rags to wipe the two bloody faces clean.

"My father was stubborn and sometimes unreasonable

like your father, Ralph. But we're not, and we are going to all be friends. Aren't we?"

Ralph nodded a little. "You and Billy Joe Meeker are cattlemen and cowboys. You should be friends, isn't that right, Billy Joe!"

It was not a question. Mandy was demanding that they be friends.

She took the now half-empty bucket from the cowboys and marched over and dumped it over Benjamin Fistak's bleeding head. The old man spluttered and roared in anger but quieted when Mandy knelt by his side and carefully dabbed at the wound. She spoke in such a low voice that only Clint was near enough to hear her words.

"I loved my pa and he was a lot like you, Mr. Fistak. Proud and stubborn. My uncle Milton used himself up on this ranch and died here ten years ago today. You must have been friends and neighbors. Everybody loved Uncle Milton."

Fistak winced as she touched his scalp. "He was a good man. But that one, the gunfighter, I kill him for this."

Mandy ignored that. She said, "We are going to sell you one of the finest bulls in the world and we're going to be good neighbors and friends, Mr. Fistak. We are going to get along just fine, aren't we?"

The rancher grunted. Mandy's words and manner had taken what little anger that might have remained in him after Clint's pistol-whipping. "Tell me about those big red cattle," he said grumpily. "They are fine-looking animals."

Mandy grinned. She placed the bucket down and sat cross-legged before the old man and the other cowboys and told them everything about her prized crossbred cattle.

And that's the way the Gunsmith wanted to always remember that cowgirl. So he walked to the corral, tightened his cinch, and rode south out of Montana. Toward the kindness of Mexico's bright winter sun.

J. R. ROBERTS
THE GUNSMITH

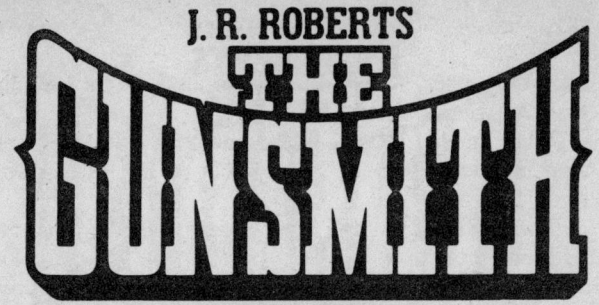

SERIES

☐ 30932-1	THE GUNSMITH	#1: MACKLIN'S WOMEN	$2.50
☐ 30930-5	THE GUNSMITH	#7: THE LONGHORN WAR	$2.50
☐ 30923-2	THE GUNSMITH	#9: HEAVYWEIGHT GUN	$2.50
☐ 30924-0	THE GUNSMITH	#10: NEW ORLEANS FIRE	$2.50
☐ 30931-3	THE GUNSMITH	#11: ONE-HANDED GUN	$2.50
☐ 30926-7	THE GUNSMITH	#12: THE CANADIAN PAYROLL	$2.50
☐ 30868-6	THE GUNSMITH	#13: DRAW TO AN INSIDE DEATH	$2.50
☐ 30922-4	THE GUNSMITH	#14: DEAD MAN'S HAND	$2.50
☐ 30905-4	THE GUNSMITH	#15: BANDIT GOLD	$2.50
☐ 30907-0	THE GUNSMITH	#17: SILVER WAR	$2.25
☐ 30908-9	THE GUNSMITH	#18: HIGH NOON AT LANCASTER	$2.50
☐ 30909-7	THE GUNSMITH	#19: BANDIDO BLOOD	$2.50
☐ 30929-1	THE GUNSMITH	#20: THE DODGE CITY GANG	$2.50
☐ 30910-0	THE GUNSMITH	#21: SASQUATCH HUNT	$2.50
☐ 30895-3	THE GUNSMITH	#24: KILLER GRIZZLY	$2.50
☐ 30897-X	THE GUNSMITH	#26: EAGLE'S GAP	$2.50
☐ 30902-X	THE GUNSMITH	#29: WILDCAT ROUND-UP	$2.50
☐ 30903-8	THE GUNSMITH	#30: THE PONDEROSA WAR	$2.50
☐ 30913-5	THE GUNSMITH	#34: NIGHT OF THE GILA	$2.50
☐ 30915-1	THE GUNSMITH	#36: BLACK PEARL SALOON	$2.50
☐ 30940-2	THE GUNSMITH	#39: THE EL PASO SALT WAR	$2.50
☐ 30941-0	THE GUNSMITH	#40: THE TEN PINES KILLER	$2.50
☐ 30942-9	THE GUNSMITH	#41: HELL WITH A PISTOL	$2.50

Available at your local bookstore or return this form to:

CHARTER
THE BERKLEY PUBLISHING GROUP, Dept. B
390 Murray Hill Parkway, East Rutherford, NJ 07073

Please send me the titles checked above. I enclose _____. Include $1.00 for postage and handling if one book is ordered; add 25¢ per book for two or more not to exceed $1.75. CA, NJ, NY and PA residents please add sales tax. Prices subject to change without notice and may be higher in Canada. Do not send cash.

NAME_____

ADDRESS_____

CITY_____ STATE/ZIP_____

(Allow six weeks for delivery.)

J. R. ROBERTS THE GUNSMITH SERIES

☐ 0-441-30951-8	THE GUNSMITH #47: THE MINERS' SHOWDOWN	$2.50
☐ 0-441-30952-6	THE GUNSMITH #48: ARCHER'S REVENGE	$2.50
☐ 0-441-30953-4	THE GUNSMITH #49: SHOWDOWN IN RATON	$2.50
☐ 0-441-30955-0	THE GUNSMITH #51: DESERT HELL	$2.50
☐ 0-441-30956-9	THE GUNSMITH #52: THE DIAMOND GUN	$2.50
☐ 0-441-30957-7	THE GUNSMITH #53: DENVER DUO	$2.50
☐ 0-441-30958-5	THE GUNSMITH #54: HELL ON WHEELS	$2.50
☐ 0-441-30959-3	THE GUNSMITH #55: THE LEGEND MAKER	$2.50
☐ 0-441-30960-7	THE GUNSMITH #56: WALKING DEAD MAN	$2.50
☐ 0-441-30961-5	THE GUNSMITH #57: CROSSFIRE MOUNTAIN	$2.50
☐ 0-441-30962-3	THE GUNSMITH #58: THE DEADLY HEALER	$2.50
☐ 0-441-30963-1	THE GUNSMITH #59: THE TRAIL DRIVE WAR	$2.50
☐ 0-441-30964-X	THE GUNSMITH #60: GERONIMO'S TRAIL	$2.50
☐ 0-441-30965-8	THE GUNSMITH #61: THE COMSTOCK GOLD FRAUD	$2.50
☐ 0-441-30966-6	THE GUNSMITH #62: BOOM TOWN KILLER	$2.50
☐ 0-441-30967-4	THE GUNSMITH #63: TEXAS TRACKDOWN	$2.50
☐ 0-441-30968-2	THE GUNSMITH #64: THE FAST DRAW LEAGUE	$2.50
☐ 0-441-30969-0	THE GUNSMITH #65: SHOWDOWN IN RIO MALO	$2.50
☐ 0-441-30970-4	THE GUNSMITH #66: OUTLAW TRAIL	$2.75
☐ 0-515-09058-1	THE GUNSMITH #67: HOMESTEADER GUNS	$2.75
☐ 0-515-09118-9	THE GUNSMITH #68: FIVE CARD DEATH	$2.75
☐ 0-515-09176-6	THE GUNSMITH #69: TRAIL DRIVE TO MONTANA	$2.75

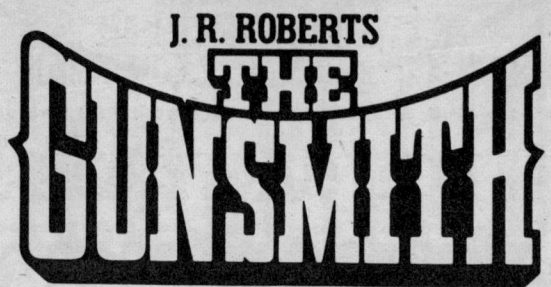

Please send the titles I've checked above. Mail orders to:

BERKLEY PUBLISHING GROUP
390 Murray Hill Pkwy., Dept. B
East Rutherford, NJ 07073

NAME_____
ADDRESS_____
CITY_____
STATE_____ZIP_____

Please allow 6 weeks for delivery.
Prices are subject to change without notice.

POSTAGE & HANDLING:
$1.00 for one book, $.25 for each additional. Do not exceed $3.50.

BOOK TOTAL	$_____
SHIPPING & HANDLING	$_____
APPLICABLE SALES TAX (CA, NJ, NY, PA)	$_____
TOTAL AMOUNT DUE	$_____

PAYABLE IN US FUNDS.
(No cash orders accepted.)

MEET STRINGER MacKAIL
NEWSMAN, GUNMAN, LADIES' MAN.

LOU CAMERON'S
STRINGER

"STRINGER's the hardest ridin,' hardest fightin' and hardest lovin' <u>hombre</u> I've had the pleasure of encountering in quite a while."
—Tabor Evans, author of the LONGARM series

It's the dawn of the twentieth century and the Old West is drawing to a close. But for Stringer MacKail, the tough-skinned reporter who is as handy with a .38 as he is with the women, the shooting's just begun.

_0-441-79064-X	STRINGER	$2.75
_0-441-79022-4	STRINGER ON DEAD MAN'S RANGE #2	$2.75

Available at your local bookstore or return this form to:

CHARTER
THE BERKLEY PUBLISHING GROUP, Dept. B
390 Murray Hill Parkway, East Rutherford, NJ 07073

Please send me the titles checked above. I enclose _____. Include $1.00 for postage and handling if one book is ordered; add 25¢ per book for two or more not to exceed $1.75. CA, NJ, NY and PA residents please add sales tax. Prices subject to change without notice and may be higher in Canada. Do not send cash.

NAME_____
ADDRESS_____
CITY_____STATE/ZIP_____
(Allow six weeks for delivery.)

The hard-hitting, gun-slinging Pride of the Pinkertons is riding solo in this new action-packed series.

J.D. HARDIN'S
RAIDER

Sharpshooting Pinkertons Doc and Raider are legends in their own time, taking care of outlaws that the local sheriffs can't handle. Doc has decided to settle down and now Raider takes on the nastiest vermin the Old West has to offer single-handedly...charming the ladies along the way.

__0-425-10017-0	**RAIDER**	$3.50
__0-425-10115-0	**RAIDER: SIXGUN CIRCUS #2**	$2.75
__0-425-10348-X	**RAIDER: THE YUMA ROUNDUP #3**	$2.75

Available at your local bookstore or return this form to:

THE BERKLEY PUBLISHING GROUP
Berkley • Jove • Charter • Ace
THE BERKLEY PUBLISHING GROUP, Dept. B
390 Murray Hill Parkway, East Rutherford, NJ 07073

Please send me the titles checked above. I enclose _____. Include $1.00 for postage and handling if one book is ordered; add 25¢ per book for two or more not to exceed $1.75. CA, NJ, NY and PA residents please add sales tax. Prices subject to change without notice and may be higher in Canada. Do not send cash.

NAME_____

ADDRESS_____

CITY_____ STATE/ZIP_____

(Allow six weeks for delivery.)